CODE NAME:

SENTINEL

By
SAWYER BENNETT

ISBN: 978-1-947212-54-1

Find Sawyer on the web!
sawyerbennett.com
www.twitter.com/bennettbooks
www.facebook.com/bennettbooks

Contents

CHAPTER 1

Cruce

JAMESON FORCE SECURITY hides in plain sight. Housed within a dilapidated old brick warehouse in the decaying Hill District of Pittsburgh, no one in a million years would guess hundreds of thousands of dollars of advanced computer equipment and servers were inside.

Or an indoor, soundproofed gun range.

Or some of the most highly trained military and law enforcement specialists in the world.

Or a research and development division that produces some of the most high-speed tech gadgets that would make James Bond's Q die from jealousy. That particular area is housed in a sub-basement level of the building I didn't even know about until a week ago. The owner, Kynan McGrath, loves his surprises.

I have to say... I love everything about my move to Pittsburgh so far. I've been here for almost six weeks, and I've had no problems settling into this place as my new home.

That's right.

I actually live at the headquarters on the fourth floor where Kynan built five small but luxurious apartments along with other communal-living areas like a gym, media and entertainment room, and a commercial-sized kitchen.

A few minutes late for a mandatory meeting Kynan had scheduled, I quickly leave my apartment. I don't bother locking my door as no one here would dare enter without my permission. It goes without saying I have implicit trust in everyone Kynan employs at Jameson because I have implicit trust in him.

I don't bother with the slow-as-molasses freight elevator at the north end of the hall. It's always faster to take the stairs. Plus, I think they're an architectural wonder in and of themselves. I have no clue what type of money Kynan spent renovating this dump, but the floating staircase spiraling upward from the first to fourth floors is a myriad of reclaimed wood and steel support cables that make the damn thing appear to float in thin air.

I take the steps two at a time down to the second floor where the offices and conference rooms are located along the perimeter. The interior walls are glass and a quick head count into the largest conference room shows I'm the last to arrive.

The huge table that takes up the middle is a work of

art. It seats twenty, and the base is made of twisted, rusted beams of steel with a thick cement slab on top. Almost every plush leather chair around the table is filled.

Kynan cuts his eyes to me as I enter, then mutters, "Glad you could take the time from your busy schedule to join us."

"Sorry," I reply with a smirk as I take an empty chair next to Bebe. "Was answering an email to the president."

Everyone whips their heads my way, but I've only got eyes for Kynan, who cocks an eyebrow. Not in skepticism, because I do indeed know the president of the United States, but more in annoyance I would just casually drop that name to excuse my tardiness.

So I appease him a bit. "He says he needs to talk to me about something important."

Kynan's expression smooths, and he sits a little straighter. "Perhaps this meeting isn't as important as talking to the president," he suggests.

Laughing, I shake my head. "He wants me to come to D.C. Asked you to come along as well. Tomorrow if we can."

I'll give Kynan credit. He's the coolest of cucumbers, and doesn't so much as flinch or blink in surprise. Instead, he just gives a curt nod. "We'll talk after this meeting."

I nod back, giving some thought as to what could be

so important that Jonathan Alexander, president of the United States, wants to see Kynan and me tomorrow in D.C. But that's going to have to wait a bit since Kynan stands from his chair to begin the meeting.

He sweeps his arm around the room. "As you can see, our conference table is getting full and we've got some fresh faces here today. I'll start off by introducing the new folks."

I look around the room, briefly glancing at each person. Since I was the first hire Kynan had made, I actually know everyone, especially since he's had me sit in on all subsequent interviews with the exception of the man sitting across the table from me, Saint Bellinger. He was hired just days after I was, but I was on an assignment watching over Kynan's fiancée the day Saint had been interviewed.

Of course, it's amazing to think I still have a job after that day, seeing as I'd managed to let Joslyn get kidnapped by a psycho stalker while she was on my watch.

On the flip side, and in fairness to me, Kynan understands Joslyn gave me the slip and doesn't fault me for losing her.

Thank fuck.

"I'm just going to go around the table to make quick introductions. I expect members who have been here longer to step up and offer guidance to the newbies."

To Kynan's immediate right sits a young black man

with a bald head and freakish bluish-gray eyes. He's sporting diamond studs in his ears, and he's impeccably dressed in a tailored suit, which is expertly cut and stitched around an impressive array of muscles. I'd peg him as a professional athlete or something, but I know that's not the case as it's not the nature of our business.

Jameson Force Security is a private agency that contracts military and security specialists for any host of reasons from recovering kidnap victims to coordinating black-op strikes against foreign enemies.

"This is Dozer," Kynan says as he points at the man. "I haven't come up with a title for him yet, but he's officially the smartest man employed by Jameson. He has an IQ of one hundred and seventy, and he turned down a very lucrative job at NASA to come join us as our head of strategy and planning as well as working with Bebe in tech. Dozer has been known to see things no one else can, which can be an invaluable resource in our line of work."

All heads now whip toward Dozer, who has suddenly become the most interesting man in the world.

He merely grins, bright white teeth flashing against his black skin, and says, "Plus... Kynan promised me I'd get to learn how to blow shit up."

This dude has it going on. Dresses like a damn movie star, has the good looks to go along with it, brains that make Stephen Hawking look stupid, *and* he wants to blow shit up. I cannot wait to have a beer with him.

My gaze moves from Dozer over to Saint, who is smirking at me. He's thinking the same thing as I am… that we're going to pull Dozer into the bromance we've had going since we started working here. We came on at the same time, and we weren't part of the original Jameson crew that moved here from Vegas. While those guys are all amazing and I'd trust with them with my life, Saint and I bonded since we were the newbies at the time.

Kynan then points to the stunning brunette sitting on the other side of Bebe. "All of you know Dr. Corinne Ellery as she did each of your psych evaluations before you were offered employment here. I'm pleased to announce she's going to be coming on board permanently with Jameson starting next month. For now, she's winding up her psychiatric practice in D.C."

"And what will the beautiful Dr. Ellery be doing, exactly?" Cage Murdock asks with a charming smile thrown her way, which she ignores. He's one of the Vegas transplants.

"She's going to be making sure all of you stay in top mental health, especially given some of the traumatic shit we're going to be getting ourselves into."

At the solid reminder we do dangerous missions, the mischievous grin slides off Cage's face.

"Corinne will have regular visitation hours and an

office on this floor. Utilize her services freely, and don't make me send you."

Nervous laughter sounds around the table.

"The guy on the end with the 'high and tight' is going to be joining us in a few weeks," Kynan continues as he points to a man who's clearly active duty. "That's Malik Fournier, and he just got out of the Marine Corps—2nd Recon. He's going to spend a few weeks with family before starting here at Jameson."

I study the man. Late twenties, I'd guess, with dark hair and hazel eyes. He's special forces, and I can tell by the look in his eyes he's seen some pretty sketchy shit. He catches my gaze and gives me a slight nod, which I return.

Welcome aboard, dude. We'll do beers, too.

"Some of you might know Malik's famous hockey brothers," Kynan continues in his crisp, British accent.

"Fournier?" Cage drawls in hesitant but hopeful surprise. "As in Max and Lucas Fournier?"

Malik grins as he nods at Cage.

"Holy fucking shit," Cage explodes, giving a Southern holler of glee as he bangs his fist on the table. Corinne Ellery about jumps out of her seat. "The Carolina Cold Fury is *my* hockey team. Mine! Two-time Stanley Cup Champions, baby."

Kynan shrugs. "I wouldn't know about that shit. We don't have bloody hockey where I'm from."

Everyone laughs because Kynan's been in the States long enough to know what ice hockey is, and he sure as hell should have heard about the Cold Fury. They're looking good for a three-peat championship this year, but they might just get upset by the new franchise team in the league, the Arizona Vengeance.

In fact, that seems to be what everyone's chattering about now. Kynan only lets it go on for about three seconds before he's banging his hand on the table to get quiet again.

"You can talk hockey with Malik later," he grumbles, then gives his attention to the dark-haired woman sitting next to me. "But for now, we've got some new tech to discuss, so I'll turn it over to Bebe."

All eyes go to our favorite hacker.

Well, our only hacker, but if there were others, none would be as beloved as Bebe. She's actually a convicted felon, but Kynan sprung her from a thirty-five-year prison sentence early. She'd been rightfully convicted of stealing sensitive military codes to launch nuclear weapons, but her reasons for doing it were understandable. Her son's life was at stake, and there wasn't anything Bebe wouldn't do for Aaron. But she loved her country, too, so she fucked over the group forcing her to steal the codes and made sure she was caught so the codes remained safe.

Our country was safe, her son was safe, and Bebe went to prison.

CODE NAME: SENTINEL

Until Kynan brought her aboard Jameson.

Bebe is officially one of the coolest people I know, and she launches into some new security feature she just installed that requires retinal scans to get into the building.

I tune her out. Apparently, I'm going to have to get my eyeballs scanned over in her lab soon, so she can fill me in then.

Instead, I fish my phone out of my pocket, then pull up the email I'd received a little bit ago.

It's not the official presidential email from the White House. No, this is a private email sent through an encrypted server.

The email address alone told me it was from President Alexander.

Cav.uh.leer1@gmail.com

"Cavalier" was Jonathan Alexander's Secret Service code name when he'd been vice president and I was assigned to his protection detail.

The email was precise, but I recognized it as coming from him. I'd worked closely with him too long not to.

Cruce,

I know I'm the one who owes you the favor, but I really need your help. This is off the books.

You saved my life once. This time, I need you to save someone whom I love deeply.

I'll send Marine One for you and Kynan McGrath in the morning.

It wasn't signed, but I knew it was from Jonathan Alexander, former vice president and current president of the United States. This wasn't a request but a command.

He'd said he was sending one of the presidential helicopters tomorrow for Kynan and me. He's equating his need to when I saved his life last year, so I know it's beyond important to him.

Of course, I never even thought about declining. One simply didn't do that when the president demanded their presence.

So I merely emailed back, *Yes, sir. See you tomorrow.*

And it looks like Jameson is going to have its first big, off-the-books contract straight from the most powerful man in the world.

CHAPTER 2

Cruce

"THE PRESIDENT WILL be with you shortly," the woman says as she backs out of the Oval Office, smiling before shutting the door behind her.

Kynan and I had been ushered here after Marine One touched down on the White House lawn. It's a helicopter ride I've made before when Jonathan Alexander was the vice president, but it still never fails to thrill. Kynan tried to act all cool about it, but I could see him practically vibrating in his seat as we came down for a landing.

For today's meeting, we'd decided on sedate suits—mine black and Kynan's a dark gray. My hands are tucked casually into my pockets, and Kynan holds onto a leather portfolio with a note pad and pen inside. Ten to one says he doesn't write down a single note. It's more of a business prop.

"What's it like to have the president indebted to you?" Kynan asks as he turns away from a portrait of George Washington above the fireplace mantel.

"He's not indebted to me." I take in the new decor President Alexander chose for his office. Steel blues and creams. Manly yet elegant. "I was just doing my job."

"Yeah, but you did it far and beyond what anyone would have expected. Put ten other agents in your spot and faced with that same scenario, he would have died those ten times."

I don't argue with him on that point. Who knows what would have happened?

All I know is my reaction speed was far greater than I had ever known possible. I learned a valuable lesson that day—I should always trust my gut instinct.

It happened just about a year ago. Alexander was still serving as the country's vice president but he was also on the campaign trail, having decided to throw his hat into the ring after then President Cary Allen decided not to run for a second term due to health issues.

We'd been at Loyola and Alexander was giving a commencement speech. After it was over and as we were walking out, one of the other agents pulled something from his pocket. I had milliseconds to react, not really understanding what I was seeing. Without thought or hesitation, I took my service pistol out and pumped bullets into my fellow agent's chest.

Turns out, it was an 8-inch shiv and the agent was a treasonous prick who was pissed at our government because of our foreign war policies. Sure, they said there was some mental illness, but fuck that. He was a fuckwad who tried to kill the sitting vice president, and he deserved to die. All there was to it.

One of the doors to the Oval Office opens—a different one from the entrance we used—and Kynan and I turn that way. President Alexander walks in, followed by two important-looking men in dark suits who are chattering to him. The president's eyes find mine, and he shoots me a welcoming but short smile as he moves to his desk. One man reminds the president he has another meeting in five minutes and the other puts something in front of him to sign, which President Alexander does without hesitation.

Then, just as quickly, the two aides melt out of the office, leaving the way they entered in a very seamless fashion.

The president moves around the desk, striding toward me. When he holds his hand out, I take it, and I'm not in the slightest surprised when it turns into a half hug rather than a formal handshake. "Damn, it's good to see you, Cruce."

"Good to see you, too, sir."

The president pulls away, giving me a chiding smile. "It's Jon. You can call me Jon."

Laughing, I shake my head. "Not going to happen, sir."

He gives my hand an extra squeeze before letting it

go.

I turn to Kynan. "Sir... this is Kynan McGrath, owner of Jameson Force Security."

A formal handshake occurs, and the president says, "I've heard incredibly good things about you from some pretty high-ranking members of Congress. Seems your company and our government work very well together."

"That we do, sir," Kynan replies crisply. "And we want to continue that tradition."

The president stares at Kynan with a fixed smile for just a moment, perhaps wondering just how far Jameson would go for its country. He then clears his throat, motioning to the two sofas sitting opposite each other.

Kynan and I sit on one while the president takes the other. While Kynan and I perch on the edge of the cushions, alert and ready to listen, the president leans back, casually crossing one leg over the other.

He picks at the pressed crease in the pant leg of his dark blue suit, brushing at the material before giving us his attention. "We've received some intelligence recently that has alarmed me on a personal level. It's vague, and some of my advisors believe it's too benign to take seriously at this time."

"Chatter?" I take a guess, referring to the term signals intelligence uses to refer to intercepted communications. There's lots of ways to get intelligence, but it's often merely by listening in on other people talking. This happens all over the world.

The president nods. "Traffic analysis picked it up out of Oman."

I blink in surprise while Kynan answers. "Not exactly a hotbed of terrorist activity as far as Middle Eastern countries go."

President Alexander nods. "Which is why my advisors don't think it's something to worry about."

"What exactly is the chatter?" I ask.

There's no mistaking the way the president's expression changes to one of personal worry, which doesn't make sense to me.

He moves forward to the edge of the couch, rests his elbows on his knees, and focuses directly on me. "Our government has contracted with The Praemium Group to work on some groundbreaking developments in fusion energy. They are remarkably close to completing some theoretical formulas that, once tested, could provide the cleanest, most efficient energy the world has ever seen."

"And the United States would own this technology?" Kynan asks.

"Technically, Praemium would own it, but our contract specifies they'd license it solely to us."

"And what would the United States do with it?" This is important toward motivation and possibly identifying who would want this technology. My mind has already made the leap that the chatter picked up was perhaps about some other country stealing the technology.

The president doesn't answer right away, and it's obvious this is perhaps information he shouldn't divulge. But then he leans forward a bit and drops his voice. "If I had my way, I'd share it with the countries that need it the most."

"I take it that's not popular with Congress?" Kynan asks.

The president chuckles. "Not with those in the other party."

"So you want Jameson to what... set up some protective services around Praemium? The goal is to prevent some digital theft of the work already created?"

Kynan turns to me, continuing his line of thought. "Because that's right up Bebe's alley. She can fortify whatever they have as well as lay traps to capture the—"

"That's not what I want Jameson for," the president interrupts, and we turn to him in surprise.

He settles his gaze on me. "In fact, it's mainly Cruce I want to hire, but he will need some backup as well."

"For what?" I ask, brows furrowing in confusion.

"The main scientist working on this is my niece, Barrett Alexander," he replies, his voice tense with worry.

"Barrie?" I ask incredulously, for some reason utilizing the nickname I always heard Alexander and his wife use when referencing her. "But I thought she worked out in California for some big think tank or something?"

"So this is off the books?" I ask.

"As far off the books as we can get," he says. "I'll be paying for this on my own, and very few people will know. Only my most trusted advisors in the White House."

"The fewer the better," Kynan suggests.

President Alexander locks his eyes on mine. Whatever he's going to ask, I cannot say no to him.

"Cruce," he begins, his voice slightly quavering. "I want you to be the one to personally protect her. She's in a secure facility during the day as she works, but she's vulnerable when not there. I want you stuck to her side when she's not at work."

I can do nothing but nod my agreement. This man I respect has just made it personal to me. While Kynan thinks the president is indebted to me, there's an element that's just the opposite. Once I became the man who saved his life, I became invested in his life as a whole. Besides, he's a fantastic leader. He loves our country, and I believe in everything he stands for. And if it's important to him that I keep his niece safe, then I'm going to oblige.

Kynan and Alexander start talking about what other resources he wants from Jameson. But I've already started thinking about what I'm going to need to adequately protect Barrett Alexander.

"She's not going to like this," the president says, the

words catching my attention.

"What do you mean?" Kynan inquires.

Alexander blows out a huff of frustration. "Barrie is… well, she's just super focused on her work. Always has been, to the point of being a bit antisocial. She's also a little too independent, but worst of all… as independent as she is, she's as equally naïve. Barrie won't believe there's a threat, or even if she does, she'll push away efforts to protect her. She doesn't like her routine being messed with."

Kynan and I exchange a look. We've dealt with difficult people in our lines of work before, but we both know when protecting someone, they have to respect our position of authority over them so we can effectively do our jobs. For example, if I were to yell at the vice president to "get down" when I was on his protective duty, he should drop to the floor without a moment's hesitation.

Sounds like Barrett Alexander might prove to be a little difficult.

The president continues. "I'd like to hit her with this immediately. As in now, if you two don't mind an overnight stay."

"We can do that," Kynan assures him.

"Sounds like I'm going to need to have my stuff shipped to me," I mutter, pulling out my phone to text Bebe to see if she would mind handling it for me. It's clear I'm not returning to Pittsburgh for the foreseeable future.

"Thought you'd left DC for good, didn't you?" Alexander murmurs with a wan smile.

"You know how much I hate driving around Dupont Circle," I joke in an attempt to put him at ease.

The gratitude is clear in his eyes and voice. "Thank you, Cruce. This means the world to me."

CHAPTER 3

Barrett

I T'S HARD TO be annoyed by Uncle Jon wanting to have dinner with me tonight. Him coming over is a rare treat because as busy as I think I am, he's a million times more so.

Seeing as he's the leader of the free world and all.

But I am a little put out because in order to get ready to host him at my DC townhome, I had to cut out of work early and I *never* leave work early.

Work is my life.

My reason for living.

The entirety of my being.

Some would say I might be a little obsessed.

But I didn't have to leave early to meet the Secret Service while they did a security sweep for safety. Not that anyone legitimately thinks I'm a threat to my uncle or there might be a rogue assassin waiting in my coat closet off the foyer in the remote chance the president happened to stop by.

No, the sweep was handled while I had my nose

buried deep in my work.

But I did have to leave early all the same because if Uncle Jon was going to take time out of his busy schedule to come see me, then I was going to make his favorite meal.

Tuna fish casserole.

No, it's not glamorous, but Aunt Janet doesn't like tuna fish—at least not from a can—so he only gets it when I can make it for him. It's about the only thing I know how to cook.

I check the timer, then peek inside the oven. The crushed potato chip topping is browning nicely, and, I have to admit... it will be nice to have a home-cooked meal. Most of my dinners are at my desk in my lab, and they consist of a granola bar or protein shake.

Which, sadly, is also my lunch and breakfast most days.

But I'm so close to a breakthrough, and I'm operating on pure adrenaline right now. I work, and I work hard. When I come home, usually around midnight, I crash hard—usually just falling face-first onto the bed. But then my alarm goes off at six, I get a run in and then a quick shower, and I'm back out the door to put in another eighteen hours.

Imagine... free energy for the entire world. Poor countries could have running water and heat, run irrigation systems for farming, and implement medical machinery in the hospitals to help diagnose and treat disease.

My doorbell rings, pulling me out of my dreams for all the good my work can do. I glance at the clock, wondering who it could be.

Seven PM.

How can it be seven already?

I'm still in the clothes I wore to work. I dress for comfort, not style, and the heather-gray leggings with a light blue button-down blouse isn't as dressy as it should be to greet the president. My dirty, off-white Chucks have certainly seen better days.

I know my hair is a mess. It always starts in a short ponytail, but my bangs eventually get in my way, so I end up shoving a bobby pin in to hold them back. It's my "hot mess" look, as my research assistant, Derrick, likes to say.

"Oh, well," I mutter, patting at the top of my head in case I've got a big rat's nest on top for some reason. I'll often lean over my computer, my fingers clutching and twirling my hair in consternation, which tends to make it an even bigger hot mess.

When the doorbell rings again, I bolt for the door, my Chucks squeaking on the hardwood floors.

I twist the deadbolt, turn the knob, and throw the door open with a smile on my face. "Uncle Jon—"

My words fall flat, ceasing when I see my uncle

standing there with two men I don't recognize. Behind them are two Secret Service agents, recognizable in their classic plain dark suits with earbuds in place.

"Barrie," my uncle says affectionately, using the nickname I despise. It's what I was called when I was a kid, but now it just makes me feel like a 1970's porn star. Still, I graciously accept his warm hug, lingering a bit since we haven't seen each other in so long.

When he pulls away, he motions the men on the porch across the threshold. "I hope you don't mind, but I brought two guests I need to introduce you to."

The two men move into my home, with the two Secret Service agents following. But when my uncle holds up his hand, they stop. "If you two will just wait on the porch."

"But, sir," one of the agents protests.

"I'm adequately protected, gentleman," is all he says before he closes the door in their faces. He gestures to the first man, a tall blond with warm brown eyes and a stylish goatee. "Barrett... this is Kynan McGrath. He owns a company called Jameson Force Security."

This mildly piques my interest, and I shake his hand in greeting.

The other man steps forward. Before my uncle can speak, he introduces himself. "I'm Cruce Britton. I work for Kynan."

A bell goes off in my head when we shake hands

because while I don't recognize his face, his name is well known to me. "You used to be Secret Service. You saved my uncle."

Cruce gives me a nod of acknowledgment, his lips curving up only slightly—seemingly more in embarrassment than amusement.

My uncle takes a deep breath, dramatically inhaling as he rubs his stomach. "Dinner smells delicious, honey. I'm starved."

Suspiciously, I cross my arms over my chest. "What's going on? Are you in danger or something?"

My uncle blinks before giving a nervous laugh. "Of course not, but how about we head into the kitchen and you serve up some of that famous tuna noodle casserole?"

"Uncle Jon," I murmur warningly. I don't have the patience to wait if there's something wrong or if I should be concerned about him.

"I swear I'm okay," he assures me, then hurries toward my kitchen. Kynan follows him, leaving me in the foyer with Cruce.

He hadn't seemed intimidating before, but now he has a certain overwhelming quality. He's taller than the other guy by a few inches, and I have to tip my head way back to see him. His hair is dark, neatly swept back, and he has a trim beard and mustache.

His eyes are disconcerting, though. A light crystalline blue that seems to slice right through me as he stares.

He's an incredibly handsome man. Intense is the word I'd use to describe him. In fact, his expression is worried, and it raises my suspicions about my uncle being in danger.

Cruce makes a motion with his hand, silently indicating I should head to the kitchen and he'll follow. Instead, I adjust my stance, putting myself in between him and the hall that leads into the kitchen.

"What's really going on?" I ask. "Why is the man who saved my uncle here? What kind of danger is he in?"

Cruce appraises me, seeming to size up my ability to handle bad news. I brace at his scrutiny, then become frustrated when his eyes cut past me to where my uncle and Kynan wait because it seems he's going to put me off.

Instead, I'm stunned when he says, "He's not the one in danger. You are, and I'm here to protect you."

♦

"I DON'T UNDERSTAND," I say for the third time. All three men sit at my kitchen table, working on second helpings of my tuna casserole. I've barely had two bites, but my stomach rebels against the idea of food right now.

My uncle shoves a huge forkful of noodles and creamy tuna into his mouth, so I turn to Kynan, who owns the company hired to protect me. "Until we can determine the full extent of what's being planned, we have to assume the worse."

"And you think they'll kidnap me?" I ask, even though they've already told me this.

"It's the most logical assumption," Kynan replies. "That they'd take you somewhere and force you to finish the formula for them."

"But I'd refuse," I point out.

"They'd force you," Cruce says quietly, and the surety in his voice causes a tremor to run up my spine.

But no... I can't accept what they're saying. "It doesn't make sense. The formula is nothing without the ability to test it, and fusion reactors can't be bought at Target."

"True," Kynan says, but then proceeds to burst my bubble. "But there are plenty of foreign countries and terrorist organizations with the funding and access to the materials needed."

"And you want to hire protection for me?" I ask. This time, I direct my question at my uncle, who is still chewing the last bite he'd taken.

He swallows, then wipes his mouth on a napkin. "It's only until we can ferret out who these people are and shut them down. But until then, I can't take a risk—"

"I'm already protected at work." I say, cutting him off with an impatient wave of my hand. "And if you need to assign someone to escort me home, that's fine. But I don't need—"

"It's already been decided, Barrie," my uncle says, his high-handedness making my teeth gnash together.

"I'm an adult, Uncle Jon," I snap. "You can't dictate—"

"I am your president—the one who ensures your company gets the funding for your research," he growls, leaning toward me from his chair. "And you will accept the security I'm hiring."

I swallow hard, fuming but silently admitting he just intimidated the shit out of me.

His face softens, though, and he reaches out to take my hand. "But indulge an overprotective uncle, will you, honey? I'm really worried about this threat. While it might turn out to be nothing at all, you are going to help an old man sleep at night if you just let these men protect you for a while. Okay?"

I let out a long, submissive sigh.

Because after hearing him put it that way, I'd never do anything to cause him distress.

"Okay, fine," I mutter as I pick up my fork and stab a noodle. "But what exactly does this 'extra protection' look like?"

"We're going to have two men escort you to and from work each day," Kynan answers for him. Of course, we'll tweak our plan over the next twenty-four hours, and I suspect Bebe and our new hire, Dozer, will be involved as well. "Same at work... two men outside your lab at all times."

"But my building is secure," I say, feeling like I'm causing an awful lot of trouble and expense. "Anyone who goes inside has to have top-secret clearance and credentials to get in."

"Nothing is foolproof," Kynan replies, and I shoot a glance at Cruce. He'd finished eating, and he's just silently watching the exchange. I wonder why he's even here since he hasn't said much. "People can be bought off. Money is a powerful influencer. It wouldn't take much for someone to get into that building with the right type of planning."

I incline my head in understanding. "Okay... that makes sense. And here at my home?"

"At night, two men will patrol outside," Kynan replies before nodding his head at Cruce. "And he'll always be with you—inside and out—when you aren't at work."

"What?" I exclaim, bolting upright in my chair, my fork clattering to my plate. "No. Absolutely not. This is my home—"

"And Cruce will be staying here with you," Uncle Jonathan decries in a deep voice that is not to be trifled with. "In this world, he's the person I'd trust the most with your life, Barrett. I'm not going to be swayed on it."

My eyes cut to Cruce, and he stares right back. Not in defiance, but definitely not in understanding either. I can tell by his expression he's already accepted the duty bestowed on him by my uncle.

I push up from my chair, sullen and sounding slightly bratty. "I'll have to go change the sheets in the guest room."

"Sit," my uncle orders, and my ass hits the cushion of my kitchen chair. He gives me an understanding smile. "I know this is disruptive to you, Barrett, and how involved in your work you are. But your safety is paramount to any damn formula that will create fusion energy."

"I understand," I clip out, trying to be respectful to him as my uncle and my president. "But I don't have to like it."

Sighing, Uncle Jon reclines in his chair. "No, I don't suppose you do."

Silence ensues. Longingly, Uncle Jon stares at his empty plate while Kynan sips at his ice water. Cruce continues to stare, but I find it hard to meet his eyes.

"Don't suppose you'd pack me some leftovers to take back with me?" my uncle asks hopefully.

I can't help but snort, knowing even during the tense discussions we've had tonight, his priorities are my tuna noodle casserole. For a moment, I forget about my worries, pleased I could make him happy for a bit.

It's not until I've got Uncle Jon loaded up with the leftover casserole and he steps out onto my porch with

Kynan, leaving Cruce behind, that it becomes real to me. I now have a roommate whether I want one or not.

And to be clear… I do not. He's way too intense and distracting.

Personally, I think everyone is overreacting. My work is theoretical, and it isn't worth much until it can be tested. Which means I'm not all that valuable.

"Stay safe, Barrett," Uncle Jon whispers as he hugs me, plastic Tupperware dish gripped hard in his other hand. "I'll check in on you soon."

"I love you," I say, because I do, even though I'm not all that happy with him.

"Love you, too, kiddo," he says.

I don't wait for them to disappear into the motorcade. Instead, I shut the door softly, locking it behind me.

Turning to my guest, I nod up the stairs. "Come on. I'll show you the guest room."

Cruce is silent as he follows me. At the top, we turn right, the opposite way from my bedroom. The small guest room is sparsely furnished since I'm not big on guests to begin with. Pointing at the bed, I say, "I really don't have to change the sheets. I've only got the one set, and no one has slept on them."

"It's fine," he replies casually.

"Bathroom's right out in the hall, and there are clean towels in the closet in there," I add.

"Thank you," he replies. Those blue eyes pierce through me, causing my eyes to drop. "Think I could borrow some of your shower stuff tonight?"

My head snaps up as images of him in my shower flash before me. Beneath that suit, there are hidden layers of muscle that would look nice in my shower.

Wait! What? Where in the world had that thought come from? I haven't looked at a man like that in well... shit, I can't remember the last time. And maybe it's not those piercing blue eyes that have me disconcerted. Perhaps it's the entire package.

Cruce Britton is tall, strong, and has the face of an angel. Plus, he'd saved my uncle's life in an extremely dramatic fashion, making him the nation's hero at the time. And now he's in my house, wanting to use my shower.

"My stuff should be here tomorrow," he provides, and I blink stupidly. I'm still trying to figure out why his muscles fascinate me. He dips his head to lock eyes with mine. "When I came to Washington, I didn't know I'd be staying so I didn't pack anything. But two of my teammates, Bebe and Dozer, are driving up tomorrow with my stuff."

"It'll take two teammates to bring your stuff?" I ask. "How long are you planning to stay?"

Laughing, Cruce tips his head back. "Just a suitcase for me, but they're coming to help us do some strategy planning. In addition to protecting you, we're going to try to find out who wants you before they make a move."

"Oh," I murmur, retreating toward the door. "I'm just going to go get some toiletries you can borrow to get you through the night. I'll be right back."

I whip around, needing to put some distance between us. He's too damn magnetic, especially since I've let my mind wander places it shouldn't have.

And hey... what do you know... I just went a whole three minutes without thinking about fusion reactions.

CHAPTER 4

Cruce

D OZER CERTAINLY MADE himself right at home. His suit jacket is off and shirt sleeves rolled up as he stands at Barrett's stove. He's making chicken marsala while sporting one of her aprons. It says "Let's Get Chemical" on the front.

Kynan and Bebe sit at Barrett's kitchen table. Bebe types furiously on her laptop as I lean against the wall, flipping a kitchen knife through my fingers. It helps me think.

Dozer and Bebe had arrived around noon and Barrett opened her house to us so we could strategize the best way to keep her safe. She went on to work, escorted by two Jameson members.

Kynan called in a total of eight people—six from Vegas and two from the new Pittsburgh office, not including me. Between the eight, she would have two men with her at work and two men on the outside when she's home. I would be inside her home with her at night and protect her anywhere else outside of work hours. It's going to be awfully expensive for Jonathan Alexander, but he's sparing nothing to protect Barrett.

Past that... none of us really know what to do because of the lack of information we are dealing with. At this point, we're not even sure there's a credible threat.

It's a point I bring up again as we hash things out. "A single mention of her name by two low-level arms dealers in Oman. It doesn't make sense."

"I did some reading on fusion energy," Dozer says as he sautés chicken, seeming strangely in his element at the stove. The man has layers upon layers. "Nothing I've been able to find indicates Barrett's research would apply to weapons. So couldn't this just be a mistake?"

Sighing, Kynan leans back in his chair, his gaze going to the ceiling as he ponders aloud. "Typically, chatter is evaluated by intelligence analysts by quality and volume. We have neither here besides a single mention of her name by people who seemingly have no ties to energy terrorism."

"So why was she even flagged?" Bebe asks without taking her eyes from her screen.

"All members of the president's family are on a watch list," I say. "The minute one of their names is mentioned, it's pushed up the chain for evaluation."

"So pick up the two arms dealers and talk to them," Dozer suggests, turning from the stove. "It's your only lead."

When Kynan and I exchange a glance, Dozer picks up on it.

"What?" he asks curiously. "Is 'talk' the wrong word in this business? Should I have said *interrogate* or *torture*?"

Kynan shakes his head. "Those men are our only lead, but it's not as easy as you think to do what you're suggesting. First, we'd have to locate them, but men like that move around. Chances are they'd be in a more dangerous location than Oman. In addition to the intricacies of nabbing these guys, we'd have to find a secure location to take them to for *questioning*."

"Bottom line," I say, summarizing the main problem. "It would take weeks to plan this."

"Longer than what Barrett might have," Dozer murmurs before swiveling back to the stove.

"But we will plan it," Kynan declares as he pushes from his chair. He moves to the fridge and opens it, pulling out a bottle of water. "We don't know when or if a move will be made, so, until then, we'll arrange to go after the arms dealers. I've got Rachel putting together a team back in Vegas. Dozer... I'm going to send you there to help plan."

"Got it," he replies, pouring wine into the pan to deglaze it. I have to admit it smells damn good.

Bebe glances up from her laptop. "Well, the new security system for this house is online and working. The cameras are set to auto focus in on the faces of anyone who gets near the exterior, then run them through facial recognition software. I've programmed it to exclude the Jameson faces to cut down on redundancy."

A long, shrill beep goes off on Bebe's computer. She checks it, a slow smile coming to her face. "Barrett's home."

We hear the scrape of her key in the deadbolt lock, the front door opening, then soft steps walking toward the kitchen.

Barrett turns the corner, scanning the kitchen with uncertainty. I'd asked her to come home early so we could talk with her, and she wasn't happy about it.

I push off the wall, set the knife on the counter, and make introductions to Dozer and Bebe. Barrett nods at them before putting her briefcase and purse down on the counter.

"Hope you're hungry." Dozer beams as he moves to pour Barrett a glass of wine he'd opened earlier so it could breathe. He hands it to her, and she accepts it quietly.

Then he takes her by the elbow and escorts her to the kitchen table, gallantly pulling a seat out for her. "You just relax, and I'll dish you up the best chicken marsala you've ever tasted in your life."

"Oh, I'm not hungry," she replies, then pushes the glass of wine away. "And I've got a lot more work to do tonight, so—"

"You need to eat something," I say, my voice a little hard and commanding. She looks like she's ready to fall over. Face pale with dark circles under her eyes. Her hair is a mess. Most has fallen out of the band tying it back, and her bangs are shoved away from her forehead with a crookedly placed barrette. Oddly, despite how tired she looks, she's also incredibly beautiful in a natural, just-rolled-out-of-bed kind of way.

But she's clearly exhausted, and she no doubt needs nourishment. She only got about four hours of sleep last night, which I know because I patrolled the inside of her house several times in between light naps. She'd spent most of the night in her office, which is actually the living room of her small townhome.

Dozer is on the ball, sliding a plate of chicken marsala on the table before her. "Eat, pretty doctor lady," he says… admittedly with a great deal of charm that seems to work as she gives a wan smile and picks up her utensils.

Dozer plates up food for everyone else, pouring wine for himself, Bebe, and Kynan. I decline since I'm on duty. Everyone eats at the table except me. I prefer to take my dinner at the counter so I can observe Barrett. She methodically eats in small bites while quietly listening.

"If it will take a while to find these dealers," Dozer

says as he cuts into his chicken, "we should focus our attentions on those most likely to benefit from Barrett's research. I'd imagine foreign governments and private corporations, but my research last night seems to indicate the country making the most progress on this technology is China. Perhaps they want the final leg up."

"Or perhaps the ones that don't have any progress at all," Bebe suggests.

Dozer then launches into a long-winded dissertation on the intricacies of testing this type of theoretical research. It involves a lot of long words, but it essentially helps to focus in on the biggest suspect on the list of potentials.

Clearly, Barrett is impressed by Dozer's knowledge, which prompts her to add in her own theories. Soon, they're off and running on tangents, speaking a dialect the rest of us don't understand. Still, Bebe furiously types on her laptop, taking notes while ignoring her dinner.

"Is there any other help we can get from the government?" Bebe asks. "Any other agencies I can reach out to so I can cross reference this stuff?"

Kynan shakes his head. "It's not been escalated as a high priority at this point. The president said there are no other resources available unless we can find something to push it forward."

"So until then…" Kynan states with frustration. "We wait."

"Barrett…" I say to get her attention. She shifts to face me, eyebrows raised. "Where are all the places you go besides home and work? You could have been watched while running errands, and Bebe has a certain knack for, let's just say, hacking video feeds."

Barrett seems to ponder my question before shrugging. "Nowhere really."

I smile, understanding the need for patience. "Where do you grocery shop?"

"Online," she replies as if that's the only place to buy food. "And I have it delivered."

"Clothing?"

"Online," she replies.

"Pharmacy?"

"Online."

"You're quite the hermit," Bebe says appreciatively, as she's just the same. Always with her nose buried in her computer when she's not spending time at home with her mother and son. Despite her new freedom from prison, Bebe doesn't go anywhere. I know it's because she's always looking over her shoulder for the people who had forced her to steal the government codes.

"I work, and I sleep," Barrett says stiffly. "But I find my life fulfilling even if others don't understand it."

"Oh, girl," Bebe says, holding out her fist to Barrett, who awkwardly bumps it. "I feel you."

Barrett seems to be a bit revived after eating. Pushing

her chair back, she stands. A fond smile softens her face when she looks down at Dozer. Their matching intellects must have helped to solidify the bond the chicken marsala started. "Thank you for dinner and the genius ideas you threw out."

She nods at Bebe and Kynan before turning to me. "I'm going to get some work done unless you still need me?"

"Thank you for letting us use your house today," Kynan says as he stands as well. "We'll be getting out of here soon."

"Stay as long as you like," she replies politely, although it's obvious she doesn't like having her privacy disrupted.

"Also," he says a bit hesitantly, "don't forget you have that State dinner at the White House in two days. I just wanted you to know you'll have extra protection to and from, but Jameson isn't allowed in—"

Barrett waves him off. "Oh, I'm not going to that. Hate those things, and I've got way too much—"

"You're going," I state. Snapping her head my way, she narrows her eyes. I ignore her expression. "We need you to go. The fact you don't go anywhere and have a fairly predictable routine is going to make it difficult to identify your potential kidnappers. If your routine is disrupted a bit, we might get more chatter about you."

"Fine," she grits out, and there's no hiding her frustration. "But I think this is stupid. My theories aren't worth much. Despite what you think, this is all wasted time in my opinion."

God, I really hope she's right about that.

Barrett pivots, then marches out of the kitchen. I don't think twice as I follow her down the hall, through the foyer, and into the living room she'd converted into a sparse office. Apparently, she doesn't need much but her laptop and a large whiteboard, which she draws formulas on.

"You okay?" I ask as I stop at the entrance, leaning against the wall.

She plops down at her desk with a huff, pushing against bangs that aren't there as they're already clipped out of the way. A huge sigh escapes her, and she apologetically says, "Look... I don't mean to be ungrateful. I just don't operate well when my routine is messed up. Everything is a little stressful, and it's impacting my focus. I had a bad day at work because I couldn't concentrate, and I'm just not sure all this extra protection is needed."

"I get it," I say as I hesitantly step into the room. For some reason, it feels wrong to invade the sanctity of where her magic happens. "Your work is important to you."

"Not just important," she corrects. "It's my life."

"Like I said... I get it. Been there, done that. No

judgment from me. But you have to understand that your life could be in danger. Your uncle is doing the right thing by making these efforts to protect you. Hopefully, it will turn out to be nothing. However, if it turns out to be something, I've got your back. Nothing will happen to you on my watch, I promise."

She gives me a wan smile, then tilts her head. "Why did you leave the Secret Service? Clearly, you enjoyed it. And you were really good at it. You seemed to treat your previous career the same way I do mine... putting it at the top of your life's priority list."

I nod, smiling as I remember how easy it was to make the decision to give that job up. "I realized I'd reached all my goals in that line of work."

Barrett snorts. "You mean saving my uncle's life?"

I laugh. "Yeah... that was sort of the pinnacle of my career."

She inclines her head, her smile slipping just a little. "Well... thank you for making sure I'm safe. Despite being annoying, I do appreciate it."

"You're quite welcome," I reply before retreating a few steps, intending to leave her in peace. Just as I start to turn away, a thought hits me. "What are you going to do once you reach your goals?"

Her attention had already gone to her computer, but she gives me her regard without hesitation. She shrugs, lips curling slightly in amusement. "Get a haircut, maybe."

Fuck, I hope not. That messy bunch of blond locks is amazing just as it is.

"Or maybe take a vacation," she murmurs, her eyes going slightly dreamy. "Can't remember the last time I did that."

It should be somewhere tropical. I bet she'd look fucking fantastic in a bikini.

Her eyes refocus, and I get a sheepish smile. "Probably just get another work goal. Some new area of research. A different mystery to solve."

Yeah... from what little I know about Barrett, it's obvious she needs that in her life. Vacations and haircuts aside, she genuinely loves what she does. Apparently, she's damn good at her job if she has people wanting her intellect enough to kidnap her.

But my vow to her was real... no one will get her on my watch.

CHAPTER 5

Barrett

THE MINUTE I push my front door open while simultaneously throwing an arm over my shoulder in a wave to the two Jameson men who escorted me home from work, I'm met by Cruce.

A too-damn-attractive Cruce who's wearing a tuxedo way too well. Eyes widening, I freeze, idly wondering how long I can stare before it becomes truly awkward.

He grins in amusement, taking my briefcase and purse from my clutches before pointing up the staircase. "Go get ready. Now."

My shoulders hunch, my nose scrunches, and I can't help the low whine. "Do I have to?"

"Yes, you have to," he replies firmly.

After gripping my elbow, he deposits my stuff on the foyer table before marching me right up the stairs, not giving me time to lag. "We have to leave in twenty minutes. Whatever you have to do to make yourself presentable in that time frame, get it done."

"Bossy," I mutter as he gently but firmly propels me

into my room. He winks as he steps backward, pulling the door shut.

Rolling my eyes, I scan my room, taking in the gown Cruce must have pulled from my closet. I have quite a few since I've attended numerous presidential functions and research fundraisers over the years. Even accepted scientific awards that required a fancy dress a time or two.

I have to admit the gown he chose is a favorite of mine. Fit at the torso, it's a pale peach color with flowing layers of chiffon. Strapless with a deep cut at the top to reveal a hint of cleavage, it's elegant while still having sex appeal. As I examine it, I'm a little ashamed that my inner girly girl wants to come out and play. Cruce had even laid out a pair of high-heeled strappy gold sandals to go with it.

"Fine," I mutter. Heading to the master bath, I start stripping my clothes off as I go. "Let's do this."

I twist the shower handle to hot. While it heats, I critically assess the unfortunate mess of my hair. If I'm going to do justice to my makeup, I'm not going to have time to shampoo and style this catastrophe.

When I pull the bobby pin from the top, my long bangs flop over to the side with a weird crimp in the middle. I yank the ponytail holder out, the rest of my hair falling to hang lankly just above my shoulders.

"Just great," I gripe to the mirror, eyeballing the can

of dry shampoo that will be my best friend after my shower.

While I am not looking forward to this event and would much rather get some work done, I can't imagine attending with Cruce will be all that bad. I mean, he's certainly not hard on the eyes. Besides, since he moved into my house, I've realized I actually like talking to him.

Not that I have a lot of time to do so, but we've set up a pattern where conversation is a natural by-product. For example, after I finish my morning run—which he joins me on, of course, but talking while running is impossible—he makes breakfast while I shower. He then forces me to take ten minutes to sit and eat something nutritious like eggs or oatmeal and fruit.

During that time, we talk.

It's the same at dinner, as he's pretty much strong-armed me into coming home at a reasonable time. His logic is if I stay at work until ten or eleven PM like I normally do, I'm making it hard on the guys assigned to watch me during the day. His reasonable point I'll get the same work done at the house makes too much sense to ignore.

I don't argue because, frankly, the only reason I stay at work so late is I get lost in what I'm doing. I'll lose hours of time to my research and work without realizing how late it's gotten.

So now, Cruce calls every evening around six to tell

me to pack up and head out. I do as I'm told, because I don't want the guys watching me to suffer, and head to my house where Cruce has dinner waiting.

And we talk some more.

Over the last few days, I've learned a lot about him. He comes from a law enforcement family—his dad, brother, and sister are cops with the Chicago Police Department near where he grew up. He has another sister, too, but she—*gasp*—decided to become an interior designer.

Every day at breakfast and dinner, he regales me with stories about his family or his work in the Secret Service. He took the job with Jameson because he's in search of the next big career adventure, and he seems to love Pittsburgh.

Through some subtle digging, which probably wasn't subtle at all, I also learned he's not married, nor has he ever been in a committed relationship. That's something he and I have in common. Our distinct lack of relationships come from being too committed to our work.

I'd like to say I regaled him with interesting tales in return, but, sadly, my life is so boring I was able to summarize it while he poached my eggs yesterday.

After I'd gone through my educational accomplishments, which I'd reached at an incredibly early age, he asked, "But what do you do for fun?"

I had to really think about it, but I'd been too embarrassed to admit sex was my go-to "fun activity". Not dating. Not vacations. Not parties with other friends. If I got an itch, I scratched it physically.

Nothing sordid, of course. I usually maintained a friends-with-benefits relationship with someone likeminded whose main focus was also school and performing at an elevated level. It had always been mutually beneficial to use sex as an outlet.

Oh… I'd once smoked weed, but I hadn't liked it because it made me feel so out of control and paranoid.

I kept that bit from Cruce, too. I didn't think it made me seem cool or exciting. Instead, it felt a little pathetic.

My shower is quick, and I manage to nick myself just above my ankle while shaving. I slap a piece of toilet paper over it, then work on my hair and makeup. There's a knock on the bathroom door. Cruce's warning of, "Five minutes, Barrett," kicks me into high gear. Silently, I pray I don't come out resembling a clown.

After liberally spraying my roots with dry shampoo, I brush out my tangled hair. It ends up not looking bad at all, the various layers sticking out at oddly fashionable angles.

Except my bangs.

They're still crimped in the middle, and I can't get them to lay straight.

"Fuck it," I mutter, rummaging in a drawer to find a

jeweled barrette. I sweep my bangs back, shove the barrette in, and don't give myself a second look.

It's time to get dressed and I have no one I'm trying to impress.

I slide on a pair of nude lace panties before pulling the peach concoction over my head. The dress floats over my body. It's a little tight in the chest since it was designed to maximize cleavage and keep the fabric securely in place. Perching on the edge of the bed, I slip my heels on.

When Cruce knocks on my door, I call, "It's open."

Rising from my bed, I turn toward my full-length mirror in the corner of my room to make sure all my bits are tucked in the right places.

"Not bad," I murmur as I take myself in. Cruce's reflection shows him standing behind me, his hands clasped in front of himself.

In the mirror, I catch him running his eyes down the length of me. When I turn to face him, his eyes flash with appreciation, although they linger just a moment too long on the barrette in my hair.

Flustered, I start to reach up to touch it, but he says, "Don't. It looks perfect."

I blush, feeling the heat climbing up my chest to my cheeks, then clumsily move to my closet to grab a matching clutch.

"What's that?" Cruce asks, and I follow his gaze

downward. "Above your ankle?"

Kicking my leg out to the side to see, I blush even harder when I see the piece of toilet paper stuck to the small cut on my leg. "Shit," I mutter as I squat to grab it. "Just cut myself in the shower."

Ignoring Cruce's snort of amusement, I rise and nab my purse. When I'm finally ready, he's holding his arm out. "Shall we?"

I slip my hand into the crook of his elbow, shamelessly gripping onto the hard muscle there. If I have to spend an evening at a horribly boring State dinner, at least I'll have a handsome, engaging man by my side.

♦

"SO, WHEN THE chef brought my meal back for the third time still wrong, I knew I'd have to use the full force of my office to make a point," the Polish ambassador to some country I've never heard of says.

I grip onto the edge of the table. Not for balance, but to restrain myself from picking up my salad fork and stabbing myself in the ear with it, just so I don't have to listen to this anymore. I'm going to lodge an extremely cross complaint with Uncle Jon, letting him know in no uncertain terms that I'm never coming to another presidential event if this buffoon is the type of person I must force myself to politely converse with.

A light tap on my shoulder makes me lift my head

and I find Cruce smiling down at me. He'd been off talking to my uncle's press secretary, who'd also served with him during his term as vice president.

"Would you like to dance?" Cruce asks, holding his hand out palm up.

I consider the fork, decide a dance is a better option than stabbing myself, and place my hand in his. When he tugs me from my chair, I don't spare a glance at the Polish ambassador, even though I'll be leaving him all alone at the table. He'd managed to chase everyone else off, and I'd been the last one stuck listening to his pompous ramblings.

"I know your job is to save me from kidnappers," I murmur as Cruce leads me to the parquet dance floor in the middle of the room. "But that was quite possibly the best save of your career."

Chuckling, Cruce brings me in close. His free hand slides to rest on my lower back, and I bring mine to his shoulder. We start a passable job at a slow waltz. Because I'm not tall enough to see over his shoulder, I peek around Cruce's broad chest, spotting my aunt and uncle smiling as they watch us.

I duck out of sight, hiding my own smile. They love me so much, and they constantly fret over how hard I work. But I'm no fool—I'd already recognized my uncle ordering me to attend as his way of trying to assure I have a social life, too.

"Think we can leave soon?" I ask Cruce hopefully. "I could get in a few hours of work tonight."

Cruce's smirk is chiding. "Can't you just relax for one evening?"

I shake my head. "Nearly impossible."

"Come on, Barrett," he taunts with a laugh. "You're amazingly gorgeous tonight, the music is great, and the champagne is flowing. Live it up a little."

Gorgeous?

Amazingly gorgeous?

I blush again, feeling it all the way to the roots of my hair for some weird reason. Shyly, I drop my gaze. But Cruce isn't letting me off that easy. Next thing I know, his fingertips are pressing under my chin, forcing me to meet his eyes. It's such an intimate touch that my face gets hotter, and I'm afraid he can feel it.

His head dips closer as he murmurs, "You can take one night off, Barrett. Okay?"

His blue eyes locked on mine are mesmerizing, not as icy as I once thought. Rather, they seem all-knowing—magically understanding something about me that even I haven't quite figured out.

I'm hypersensitive to the weight of his hand on my back. The thought if I were to go to my tiptoes, I'd be close enough to kiss him flits through my mind.

Not that I would.

I mean… I'm his client. It would be totally inappropriate.

But damn… he's so handsome and well built. And… he smells so good tonight.

Just how long has it been since I've had sex?

"Barrett?" Cruce says, and I shake my head to clear it.

I blink, smiling. "Yes?"

"Had a funny look on your face," he almost whispers, expression concerned. "You okay?"

Other than shamelessly wondering what it would be like to have sex with you, I'm totally fine.

"I'm good," I say, which is a flat-out lie. But I step in just a bit closer, deciding I might as well enjoy dancing with this enigmatic man.

To my surprise, Cruce's hold on me tightens just a bit, causing my breasts to brush against his chest. I suck in a breath, but I don't read anything into it.

Nothing could ever come of it, anyway.

CHAPTER 6

Cruce

"**D**AMN IT, BARRETT," I growl as she heads out the front door. "Slow down a minute."

But she's gone, and a curse flies from my mouth as I finish lacing up my shoe.

Despite being out late last night for the State dinner, Barrett was up half an hour earlier than usual. Apparently, it doesn't matter it's Saturday and most people are enjoying a leisurely morning. To Barrett, it's just another workday.

And it's fine... I was already up, too, but I was surprised by the speed in which she completed her normal morning routine.

She always runs three miles, so I'd gotten dressed and ready for that. But I hadn't expected her to forego her first cup of coffee while informing me she didn't have time to waste on it.

"Going to that dinner last night was unproductive," she'd told me just moments ago as she placed her earbuds in and tapped her music selection on her phone, which was attached to her arm with a running band. Her voice had risen when the music came on. "I've got so much I need to catch up on."

Then she whirled around and jetted out of the kitchen before I finished my shoe.

I bolt after her even though she's relatively safe seeing as there are two Jameson men stationed outside. Surprisingly, I find it amusing and endearingly cute that she's even more serious about business this morning. It probably stems from her actually letting her metaphorical hair down last night.

She might want to deny it—even try to purge it by running head-first into her work as an escape, but Barrett had relaxed last night. I've never seen her that way. Quick to laugh—she's got a great fucking laugh—and she'd been a pleasure to dance with. I'd been lucky enough to be her partner several times.

But it had been more fun just to talk to her in a loose, casual environment.

Once, when Barrett went off to the powder room, the president had even sidled up to me and slyly whispered, "You're good for her, Cruce." I'd stiffened, not liking the implication in his words.

"Just doing my job, sir," I'd replied, making sure my tone stayed flat and detached.

When he'd snickered, I felt like punching him for being so astute, but the idea of spending the rest of my life in prison had kept my fists clenched at my side. Clearly, Jonathan Alexander saw what I was feeling.

I'd been having a wonderful time with Barrett, which could only spell disaster.

While she'd woken up this morning ready to blaze new trails in her research, I'd opened my eyes and immediately wanted to put distance between us.

Of course, not the literal kind since I'm bound to my duty as her protector. I take the front porch steps two at a time, then make a sharp right to follow her normal route. She's only half a block in front of me, her short blond ponytail bobbing as she sets her pace.

My legs are longer, though. By the time she reaches the first intersection, I've already caught up to her.

But I don't run beside Barrett. I always hang back about five yards so I can keep an eye on our surroundings. Her residential neighborhood is quiet as expected on a Saturday morning—the usual bustle of an early weekday absent. A few people speed-walk toward the closest Metro station, cars creep slowly by, and a couple of early risers are getting in their runs. Today, there's no wait time to cross at intersections, so we maintain a steady pace.

I've never had difficulty focusing on my job. Case in point... I shot a man dead without a moment's hesitation because I was so attuned to Alexander's safety I hadn't thought twice about it. It's why I'm so good at what I do.

Admittedly, though… it's a bit of a struggle to keep my eyes off Barrett's ass as she runs in front of me. Let's face it… she has a phenomenal ass. Seeing the relaxed, fun side of her last night while she'd been so elegantly sexy in her dress, makes her delicious curves harder to ignore.

We make it three more blocks. Per her usual route, Barrett hangs a right which leads us into a small park. The winding path is bordered with cherry trees that dropped their blossoms several weeks ago.

We make one loop around the park before Barrett starts the backward route to her townhome.

I follow along—keeping my eyes firmly off her ass— and constantly scan our surroundings as we chew up the blocks back to her place.

It's why I note the silver van as it approaches from our right at the intersection up ahead. It eases to a full stop, then turns right, now traveling in the same direction we are but about twenty yards ahead. The side of the van says "Stanley Movers".

After pulling into a parallel parking spot, the passenger gets out. He's wearing a cream-colored jumpsuit, the type of uniform movers might wear. Hurrying to the rear double doors, he opens them and reaches inside. He pulls out one of those quilted moving blankets that protects furniture, then starts to unfold it. I pick up my pace only slightly, not convinced this is anything but a couch being moved.

Barrett speeds up a bit now since we're only five or so blocks from her home. She likes to kick it at the end, and I adjust accordingly.

Just as she approaches the van, the man at the rear does something strange. His dips his head and turns so he can rub his chin on his shoulder, but I'm alarmed when I realize it's a ruse to look at Barrett as she approaches. His eyes are hard, determined, and locked onto her. When he straightens and pivots to face her, I note he's holding a wooden bat in his hand.

This lets me know he's not stupid. He's going for the quick knock out rather than using something slow acting like chloroform. Despite what's portrayed in the movies, chloroform shouldn't be the first choice to render someone unconscious.

Of interest, the man doesn't seem to notice me running just a few yards behind her and off to the side a bit. It tells me his research isn't any good, and he has no clue I've been assigned to protect her.

Barrett has no idea of the danger now a mere few feet away. The man takes a step toward the curb, the driver of the van watching in the rearview mirror briefly catches my attention. I reach my right hand across my stomach, snake it quickly under my t-shirt, and pull out my Ruger 9mm from my canvas chest holster.

It will do no good to warn Barrett. Her music is blaring, and she won't hear me.

I don't feel magnanimous enough to give the man warning. Besides, I don't want him bolting away. I merely stop in my tracks, take a deep breath, and aim at his left thigh. When I slowly squeeze the trigger, I feel the gun jump. The man crumbles to the sidewalk, falling right in Barrett's path.

The wounded man flopping right at her feet would be comical if it weren't so fucking dangerous. She screams, scuttles sideways, and actually careens into the concrete railing of the porch steps to a house. The driver of the van puts it in gear and guns it, tires spinning wildly and throwing smoke before it peels out, leaving his fallen comrade behind.

I don't waste any time, sprinting to the man now writhing on the sidewalk as he holds both hands to the bloody hole in his leg. My gun stays trained on him, but I spare a fleeting glance at Barrett. Wide-eyed, she gapes, taking it all in.

She pulls her wireless earbuds out, and they fall to the ground as she takes a tentative step toward us. I shake my head at her. "Call Kynan."

Barrett pulls her phone out of her arm band. I'd programmed Kynan's number as well as Bebe's and Dozer's in it.

"Not 9-1-1?" she asks hesitantly.

"No," I reply calmly as I keep my eyes locked on the perp. They've probably already been called by an alarmed neighbor who heard the gunshot. "Kynan."

She doesn't question me, but immediately starts dialing. I'm vaguely aware of people coming out of their brownstones to huddle in robes on their front porch. But I don't pay any attention since the man on the ground is screaming, "You fucking shot me, you asshole. Why?"

"Because I don't take kindly to kidnappings," I say calmly.

"Kidnappings?" the man screeches. "I'm here to move a bedroom set."

"Oh yeah," I reply sharply. "Then where did your partner go?"

"Probably got the fuck out of dodge once you started shooting," he yells.

I'm not buying it. The wooden bat is laying in the street. I'd bet my life he'd been making a move for Barrett. No regrets on my decision to shoot first and ask questions later, but time is of the essence. The police aren't going to take kindly to what I did.

"Kynan wants to talk to you," Barrett says. She shuffles sideways toward me, making a wide berth around the man on the ground.

Clearly understanding I need to keep my gun trained on the man as I have no clue if he's armed, she holds the phone up to my ear. I keep it short and simple. "It was an attempted kidnapping. I shot one in the leg. We need to take him into our custody so we can question him. Make it happen."

"Got it," Kynan replies without any hesitation, completely accepting my take on the situation.

When I nod at Barrett to pull the phone away, she scuttles backward to a safer distance. At that moment, the two Jameson staff in charge of the exterior of her house come running up. I assume they heard the gunshot.

I give them quick orders to search the man. Within moments, his hands are zip-tied behind his back. A kindly neighbor hands one of my men a kitchen towel, and it's pressed to the perp's wound, which appears to be non-lethal—*thank fuck*. I don't want the asshole dying from blood loss before we can question him.

The next half hour is a cluster fuck. The Metro police arrive first. Clearly, they only see me—with a gun—and a wounded man on the ground. With slow movements, I quickly give up my weapon while explaining the situation. It doesn't stop me from getting handcuffed, though, while the cops attend to the man's wound. Barrett is escorted back to her house by my Jameson men with strict orders to stay inside with weapons drawn until I can get there.

I'm nervous when an ambulance shows up next, worried the perp's going to be whisked away, but right behind it is a dark, unmarked car. Two Secret Service agents emerge from it. I don't recognize either, but they have a short conversation with the EMT workers before heading toward the cops.

Their conversation is remarkably brief, and the police turn astonished eyes toward me.

Next, the handcuffs are removed and I'm meeting SS Agent Mike Hamricher. We shake hands, and he tells me, "I was sent here on orders of the president. The ambulance will take that guy wherever you want."

Said guy is being loaded into the back of the vehicle. I ask Hamricher, "Will he survive a trip to Pittsburgh?"

Shrugging, he gestures to the EMTs "Let's find out."

Turns out, the bullet went clean through the muscle of his thigh, although I certainly wasn't trying for that. Just wanted to bring him down without using a kill shot. I leave Hamricher in charge of the final details of what will go in the police report and directing the transport of the suspect to the Jameson offices in Pittsburgh. If Hamricher thinks any of this is strange or intriguing, he doesn't show it. I have no clue what President Alexander ordered him to do, but I'm grateful for Kynan's quick work getting this organized.

After retrieving my pistol from the police, I give a final handshake to Hamricher and head to Barrett's brownstone.

One thing is for sure—she's not safe here anymore.

CHAPTER 7

Barrett

SITTING AT MY desk in my living room office, I stare at my folded hands. One of the Jameson guys is at the front door, peering out the side window with his gun drawn. The other is somewhere at the back of the house.

For the first time in what seems to be forever, I'm not even thinking about work. No interest in my formulas or dreaming about energy.

Nope. All I can think about is the crack of a gunshot that drowned out the music in my ears and a man falling helplessly to my feet with a hole in his leg. When I'd looked over my shoulder at Cruce, I'd been terrified by the expression on his face.

Cold, hard, vindictive.

He shot that man.

Deep down, I know he did it to protect me, and there is comfort in that. But the fact I am in serious danger comes crashing down on me. I don't think I actually believed it until now.

I focus on my fingers, which are tightly laced. When

I loosen them, my hands immediately start shaking, so I clasp them hard together once again.

The front door opens, the Jameson man steps backward, and Cruce enters. I can't even appreciate how great he looks in a gray t-shirt and loose shorts with his strong, tanned legs. When he sweeps his gaze around, it finally lands on me.

He jerks his head, indicating I should come to him. "We need to get packed up."

I slowly rise from my desk, my legs feeling rubbery. "Packed up?"

"You can't stay here," he says, impatiently striding toward me. He grabs my arm, then leads me from the room and up the staircase while my head spins with the implications.

"But I can't leave," I mutter as I blindly follow. "My work."

"You can work from your laptop," he snaps, steering me right into my bedroom. He releases his hold on me, rifles through my closet, and pulls out a suitcase, which he tosses on my bed. When he sees I'm not moving, he barks, "Let's go, Barrett. Get whatever shit you need from the bathroom."

I feel like I'm in a dream, things swirling slowly through my fogged brain. I'm having a tough time comprehending the situation. I watch as Cruce goes to my drawers and starts pulling clothes out, tossing them in the suitcase.

He snaps his head up, eyebrows furrowed, and growls. "Barrett... let's go. Move."

"Don't bark at me like I'm a soldier in your army," I finally manage to say, although my feet start moving toward the bathroom.

He doesn't reply, and I let it go. I have no clue what the rush is, but what I do know is Cruce just most likely saved my life, so if he's feeling an urgency to leave, I need to respect that.

I bend over to grab my makeup case from under the cabinet. Suddenly, pain slices across my left rib cage.

"Damn," I hiss as I straighten, pulling my tank up so I can see what in the blazes caused it.

The entire left side of my ribs is scraped with mottled bruising underneath. It all comes back in a rush—when Cruce shot the man and he fell into my path, I'd careened out of control and ran into a cement porch railing. I'm not sure I felt it then, but I can clearly see— and feel—the results of the impact now.

"Jesus," Cruce says from the doorway, his eyes pinned on my ribs. He rushes toward me, pulling my tank up even higher so he can examine it. The bottoms of my breasts are exposed, covered in a sweaty bra, but I don't care.

I'm beyond caring about petty stuff right now.

"You ran into the porch railing," he murmurs, apparently having seen me do that. Amazing, given he was all busy with shooting and keeping his attention on the man who tried to kill me.

Cruce lets out a heavy sigh as he gently pulls my tank down. His hands go to my shoulders, and he gently squeezes. "I'm going to go get some ice for that. Why don't you jump in the shower and clean up the scrapes?"

I nod, unable to speak. I prefer the hardened, all-business Cruce. This softer version makes me feel like crying for some reason.

Another squeeze to my shoulder and he starts to turn away.

"This is real, isn't it?" I ask, my voice quavering slightly.

He nods. "Very real. And the fact whoever wants you was willing to try to snatch you off a public street means they are not operating with subtlety. They want you at any risk, and I expect they're going to come back sooner rather than later."

"Where will we go?" I ask.

"Pittsburgh for now," he replies. "We'll figure it out from there."

An idea strikes me. "I have stuff at my office I need to get."

"Tell me exactly what it is, and I'll send men over now to get it," he replies.

After I give him the details, he leaves me in my bathroom. I stare at myself in the mirror for just a moment before I spring into action. My ribs feel okay as long as I don't bend in the hurt side's direction. I take a shower as Cruce ordered, soaping up the scrapes and gently drying them after. When I'm done, I run a brush through my wet hair, but otherwise ignore it.

Since we're traveling, I dress in a pair of black leggings and a loose, off-the-shoulder t-shirt along with my trusty, yet squeaky Chucks. They give me slight comfort as I'm getting ready to head off into the unknown, terrified my life is now in danger. My safety has now become more important to me than my work.

A soft knock at my door announces Cruce. He has an ice pack, and he hands it to me. I put it up against my ribs, thankful for the t-shirt in between to ward off the cold.

"You ready to go?" he asks.

I nod, pointing to the small tote I'd filled with my toiletries. I have to trust Cruce packed appropriate clothing for me, since my large suitcase was filled and zipped tight when I got out of the shower.

He moves for the door, but I reach out and grab his arm. Curiously, he meets my eyes.

"Thank you," I tell him softly. "For saving me out there."

"Just doing my job, Barrett," he replies gruffly, then starts to turn away from me.

Holding tightly to him, I force his attention back to me. I squeeze his forearm for affect. "In polite circles, when someone thanks you, you really should say 'You're welcome'."

Cruce's lips curve upward, and I'm shocked when he moves into my space. His hand goes behind my neck, and his face dips close to mine. Tilting his head slightly, he replies ever so softly, "You're welcome."

I smile, knowing this is more than a job to him. Just as with my uncle, Cruce cares about his work to such a degree that failure is never going to be an option. He goes above and beyond. In this moment, I realize I'll always be safe with him.

♦

SOMETHING IS SHAKING me, and I hear Cruce's voice pierce the fog of sleep. "Wake up, Barrett. We're here."

I blink slowly, sit up straight, and bring my hand to the seat belt to release it. I don't remember falling asleep, but we're now in a dark, basement-type parking lot. There's not much ambient light, but enough to see the walls are covered with graffiti and garbage is strewn over the cement floor.

"Where are we?" I mutter, rubbing my eyes.

"Jameson headquarters," he replies before exiting the vehicle.

I wrinkle my nose, not all that impressed with what

I'm seeing.

I get out and follow, wondering what kind of business is located in a dump like this. And for that matter, I wonder if Uncle Jon has ever been here. All my confidence in Cruce starts to ebb seeing as how he's led me into some seedy underbelly of Pittsburgh.

At a massive steel door, Cruce opens a panel, hits a button, and then steps in close. I'm stunned when a green laser shoots outward to scan his eyes. There's a clicking sound, and Cruce opens the door.

From that amazing bit of technology, I expect to enter into a technologically advanced fortress. Instead, we enter into what looks like an old abandoned warehouse. Dirty concrete flooring, garbage all over, and even more graffiti over the red bricked interior. The arched windows, while lovely, are covered in dirt so thick barely any light shines through.

I follow Cruce across the floor to the opposite side of the building where there's a freight elevator. Another eye scan has the scrolled gate unlocking, and we step inside. It creaks and groans its way up one floor. As it comes into view, I'm absolutely astounded by what I'm now seeing.

Sleek hardwood floors, refurbished red brick walls, and high-end furniture. I get a glimpse of desks and computers before we continue up. There's not much to see on the third floor except more gleaming hardwood floors and a long hallway that has several closed doors.

We go up one more floor, which by my account is the 4th if you count the parking garage as a basement level. The elevator comes to a shuddering stop. The grate opens, and we step into what looks like a huge living room.

Large couches, plush recliners, and a huge wall-mounted TV make up a cozy sitting area. To the right is a massive industrial kitchen. Beyond that, a short hallway ends in a T-intersection.

"There you are," a woman's voice says, and I turn in that direction.

My jaw drops as I take in the blonde walking my way, her arms outstretched and an empathetic expression on her face.

Before she reaches me, I mutter to Cruce, "Holy shit... that's Joslyn Meyers."

I may mostly lock myself away in a world of energy and physics, but one of my pleasures is music and Joslyn Meyers is a favorite of mine. She's an A-lister who can both act and sing, and I have every one of her albums.

The petite woman wraps me in a big bear hug, then she pulls away to scan me with almost motherly concern.

"Clearly, you know Joslyn," Cruce says dryly. "She's Kynan's fiancée and the mother hen of the group."

That's right. I remember seeing something online about her taking a break from show business, but I never would have thought she'd be camped out in Pittsburgh as the den mother for Jameson Force Security.

"Kynan's waiting for you downstairs in the large conference room," Joslyn tells Cruce as she wraps her arm around my waist. "I was just starting dinner, so maybe Barrett can stay up here with me and help."

Cruce nods gratefully, which means he doesn't want me involved in whatever conversation they might have. Somehow, I think it might have to do with the man they took prisoner. I imagine they think it might be too much for my delicate sensibilities, and I'm pretty sure I agree.

"I'll have her luggage sent up," Cruce tells Joslyn. "She'll be staying in my apartment."

Joslyn blinks at this news, as do I. He lives here?

Cruce turns to me. Once again, he steps in and puts his hand behind my neck. I take that as his signal he wants my full and undivided attention. My eyes lock onto his blue ones.

"Have Joslyn make you an ice pack and get it on those ribs again, okay?"

"Okay," I murmur, feeling as if maybe I'm more than a job to him.

"Good girl," he replies, then his hand falls away and he walks to the elevator.

I glance at Joslyn, whose gaze follows Cruce. She has a pensive look on her face, and I can tell his behavior around me perplexes her for some reason.

"Cruce seems like a nice guy," I say to get her attention as the elevator descends.

"He is," she replies brightly, but she doesn't take my bait to talk about him further. Instead, she starts toward the kitchen and motions for me to follow. "I was going to make a lasagna for dinner. It's a good go-to to feed a crowd."

"Crowd?" I ask.

"Me, you, Kynan, Bebe, Cruce, and Saint. Not a huge crowd, but those men can eat."

"Where's Dozer?" I ask. Based on his chicken marsala, he should be up here cooking for us.

Joslyn walks over to the freezer, then pulls out a gelled ice pack. "He's in Vegas helping them put a plan together to nab the arms dealers who mentioned your name."

"Should that still be done now since we have one of the guys who actually tried to kidnap me?" I ask as she wraps a tea towel around the ice pack and hands it to me.

Joslyn shrugs. "It would seem that might be a waste now, but I bet that's on their discussion agenda. I'm sure they'll fill us in at supper. Now, have a seat. Would you like a glass of wine?"

I manage to get on one of the high barstools at the oversized counter separating the kitchen and living area, then place the pack against my ribs, which don't even ache that much. "Wine would be great."

While Joslyn pours us each a glass, I look around curiously. "So... what is this place?"

"This is the communal living area. This floor has five apartments. Each one has its own living area and small kitchen, but Kynan wanted something where everyone could gather as a team to cook or hang out if we wanted to."

"That's very progressive," I murmur appreciatively. I imagine teamwork building is a must in this line of business.

"That's my man," Joslyn replies with a soft smile. Wow! If I could paint a picture of what being in love meant, it would be the expression she's wearing right now.

For some odd reason, it makes me feel sad I've never worn that look before. I wonder if Cruce has.

Which is even odder. I have no business wondering about him in that manner.

Still, I can't deny I like it when he puts his hand on my neck to make sure I have eyes only for him.

Or that I feel very safe and secure when I'm in his presence.

And damn... last night at the State dinner, I didn't want the evening to end. I got lost in talking to him, dancing with him, and laughing together.

Yes, I am just a job to him, but it doesn't mean he's not easy to like.

I mean, way too easy to like.

CHAPTER 8

Cruce

I HEAD DOWN to the first-floor basement. Kynan chose to keep its appearance abandoned and filthy as a deterrent in case anyone managed to get past the alarm system and fortified locks on the doors. He wanted any intruder to only see what this placed appeared to be... unoccupied and worthless. It wouldn't keep someone at bay from exploring for long, but it would give the occupants time to react.

Eventually, I imagine he'll do something down here, but for now, I don't give it much thought other than to head to the east end of the building. Joslyn told me Kynan was in the conference room on the second floor, but he'd texted me to come straight to Sub Three.

Apparently, this warehouse was originally built with underground food and beverage storage, which used the natural chill of subterranean temperatures. There are three floors below the first floor, but they don't run the entire length of the building and Sub One butts up against the garage level. Each floor is about fifty-feet-by-a-hundred feet and can be accessed by a separate freight elevator on the east side. Only Sub One has been renovated, and it's where Research and Tech will operate once Kynan makes further hires. I expect Dozer and Bebe will have a lot of say in who comes to work in that division.

I take the rumbling boxed mode of transportation down, wishing I'd worn a jacket as it's fucking cold. I'd guess maybe high forties, but in the darkened space with concrete flooring it seems colder.

Kynan and Saint are waiting for me.

Grinning, Saint holds out a fist. "Excellent shot, bro."

I bump my fist against his. "Thanks." Turning to Kynan, I ask, "You get anything from him yet?"

"Not much," he says, but he doesn't sound the least bit disgruntled about it. "Took a bit of time to get him patched up. Poor Corinne had to put stitches in him, and she bitched about it the entire time."

"She's a psychiatrist," I point out. "The last time she treated an actual body was probably medical school."

"I'll give her a fucking bonus," Kynan mutters as he stalks across the barren space. "But he gave his name—Keith Spire—and Bebe did a short background check. He lives in Bethesda, he's single, works at a garage, and has some minor convictions like petty larceny."

There's a door on the opposite end of the room, and

he opens it to give me a peek inside. In the center of the small area, the man I shot sits in a chair. His hands are tied behind his back, his legs to the chair. Someone dressed him in a pair of sweatpants and a white t-shirt. There's a black blindfold tied around his eyes, and his head pops up at the sound of the door opening.

"Who's there?" he demands angrily. "I'm fucking cold and hungry. I've been shot. I demand to have my phone call. I want my lawyer."

"Shut the fuck up," Kynan snarls before slamming the door shut. We take a few steps away so there's no chance our voices will carry to him. "So far, he's denied knowing any deep details of why Barrett is a target. Swears he and his partner were hired anonymously, and they were only told to grab her and bring her to a location that would be given to them once they had her. They were paid five thousand dollars up front, and they would get another five thousand on delivery."

"Do you believe him?" I ask skeptically.

Kynan shrugs. "We haven't had a lot of time with him yet. Saint and I did the good cop/bad cop routine a bit, but he's stuck to the same story that he doesn't know anything."

"Give me ten minutes with the fucker and I'll get the information," I growl.

Chuckling, Kynan claps me on the shoulder. "As much as I'd like to, you know we can't rough him up.

We're walking a fine line here, seeing as how we've essentially kidnapped the kidnapper."

"With the president's approval," I point out, since Jonathan Alexander is the one who made all this possible.

"That's off the books," Saint points out. "And even if it weren't, we can't put that on his doorstep."

"What can we do to get him to talk?" I ask. I'm hoping waterboarding is on the list.

"Not much," Kynan replies with a slight amount of bitterness. "Sleep and food deprivation. We'll keep him uncomfortable… hence the cold room."

"What about sodium thiopental?" I suggest. It's a drug that slows down the brain to make performance of high-functioning tasks difficult. Some call it a truth serum, but it doesn't actually make people tell the truth. It just makes it extremely difficult to keep up a stream of believable lies.

"Nope," Kynan replies. "Not only do we not have access to that, but that would also be considered a physical assault by the authorities."

"Can he be offered a reduced sentence in exchange for information?" Saint asks, which is also a good question.

Kynan shakes his head. "Not right now. This man's a ghost to law enforcement. We don't have access to that type of authority."

"So essentially, it's a wait-and-see type of thing," I

mutter, scrubbing my hand through my hair. I glance over my shoulder at the door, wanting just a few minutes alone with him.

A thought strikes me, and I turn to Kynan and Saint. "Either of you bothered by the fact this guy is American?"

"It crossed my mind as odd," Kynan admits.

"It is, given the original chatter was in Oman by two Middle Eastern arms dealers," Saint adds. "Spire refuses to identify the driver, though."

"Driver was blond," I tell them, "so most likely American, too."

"Doesn't mean it wasn't a foreign government or organization," Kynan interjects as he starts leading us back to the elevator. "They could have hired Americans for this part to throw us off."

That's plausible.

But that's all we have at this point—supposition.

"Whoever hired these guys has to be nervous we have one of them," Saint says as we reach the elevator. When he opens the metal gate, we step in. "It could mean they'll back off."

"Or..." I suggest a different alternative. "If they really hired two guys to do the kidnapping but kept themselves anonymous, they've got nothing to worry about. They'll come after Barrett again."

"You're safe here," Kynan assures me as we start to

ascend upward.

I consider his words for a moment, but they don't sit right. "No offense to what you've got here, but I'm not sure we would be safe. Too many people already know the strings that were pulled to keep Spire in our custody. The police on scene, the Secret Service agents, and the ambulance transport. And while I know this facility is secure, we don't know the lengths to which these people will go to get their hands on Barrett. Despite their first poor attempt at snatching her, we have to assume the worst. That because her knowledge is worth a lot of fucking money, they'd be willing to do whatever it takes to get her. They'll step up their game."

"What are you saying?" Saint asks.

The elevator comes to a lurching stop on the first-floor level, and we exit. I turn to face them. "I'm saying I'm not going to put the people here in jeopardy. Say they send in an advanced strike team… assault with RPGs or some other type of explosives to blast their way in. Too many people are at risk."

"That's highly unlikely," Kynan drawls.

"Agreed," I say, tilting my head in acknowledgment. "But are you willing to put Joslyn at risk?"

His face clouds, then darkens before he grits out, "Point taken."

At that moment, his phone chimes a text and he pulls it out for a quick glance. His lips curve upward.

"Speaking of the hottie, Joslyn says we need to head up for dinner."

"I'm starved," Saint says, and I add a grunt of agreement. I drove straight here from D.C. without stopping except for gas.

"Where's Bebe?" I ask as we head over to the other elevator that will take us up to the inhabited space.

"Went home a little bit ago," Kynan replies. "It's Aaron's birthday."

"Shit," I mutter, having forgot that little tidbit. I'd planned to buy him a few Xbox games, but it totally slipped my mind with everything going on with Barrett.

"Joslyn covered you," Kynan says with a grin.

I let out a sigh of gratitude. "I could kiss her."

"I could kill you," Kynan replies with an evil smile.

I grin. "Noted."

In the communal area of the fourth floor, we find Joslyn pulling a bubbling lasagna out of the oven and Barrett mixing up a salad in a wooden bowl. She shoots me a worried look, and I jerk my chin to indicate I want to talk to her privately.

She puts the salad tongs down, then wipes her hands on a towel. Kynan moves around the corner, giving her a nod of greeting before going to Joslyn and wrapping her in a hug while she irritably snaps she's going to drop the lasagna. Saint just heads to the fridge, then snags a beer.

I hold my hand out, Barrett takes it, and I lead her

down the hallway past my apartment and the others to the intersection at the end. The laundry facilities are to the right, and a small staircase that leads up to the roof is to the left.

The roof is my favorite place, and Joslyn made it a paradise. She's covered most of the surface with potted plants and trees. The perimeter is bordered by a four-foot wall so no one can see up here from street level. There aren't any taller buildings around to indicate we've got a miniature jungle up here. There are two sets of patio dining furniture as well as boxed vegetable gardens Joslyn started.

I lead Barrett over to one of the tables, and she sits. I take the seat beside her, sitting reassuringly close.

I start by filling her in on the things I know she'll be most curious about. "The man who tried to kidnap you is American, but that's about all we know. He swears he doesn't know who hired him—that it was anonymous."

"Do you believe him?" she asks.

"I don't know, since I haven't been able to talk to him. Kynan's going to continue to work on him, though."

She mulls over it before nodding her understanding. "What now?"

"Now, you and I have to leave," I tell her. "Too many people know we're here, and we don't know who wants you. So we have to go off-the-grid."

"Off-the-grid?" she murmurs.

"Somewhere no one will know where we are or how to find us," I clarify.

"My uncle?"

I shake my head. "No one but Kynan and maybe a select few here at Jameson."

Barrett's eyes cloud with frustration. "For how long? When exactly will I get my life back?"

My hand goes to her knee and I give it a squeeze. It doesn't seem too forward, and Barrett doesn't react negatively to my touch. "I'm sorry. I know this is hard on you, but my job is to keep you alive. If we're lucky, Kynan will learn something from this guy. We also still have the team in Vegas pursuing leads with the arms dealers who originally mentioned you."

"Or they can make another move on me," she suggests softly, her gaze moving toward a pot of pretty yellow flowers. The tone of her voice tells me that scenario is one she does not want to happen.

This is good, as she understands going on the run and hiding is our best bet to keep her safe.

She continues to stare for a moment before focusing on me. I get an agreeable but tired smile from her. "Okay. Whatever you think is best."

I rise from the table, offering her my hand again. She takes it easily, and I tug to pull her up. Regretfully, I let go the minute she has her feet under her. Together, we return to the kitchen.

Joslyn already has the table set. She, Kynan, and Saint are seated and waiting for us. Joslyn introduces Barrett and Saint while I grab a few bottled waters from the fridge. Joslyn serves up steaming plates of gooey lasagna. I forego a salad because... why would I want rabbit food when I can eat cheesy goodness?

We engage in general small talk, and Saint goes into overdrive trying to charm Barrett. Makes me want to punch him so I concentrate on my food.

"I've got an idea," Joslyn says while we tuck into our meals. "About where you and Barrett can go."

I pop up, fork full of cheese and pasta paused in midair. "Where's that?"

"How about a private island in the Caribbean?" she suggests with a triumphant smile. "Accessible only by boat or helicopter, private and security conscious."

I cock an eyebrow at Kynan, because while I love Joslyn for putting her thinking cap on as well as getting a birthday present for Aaron from me, she's not a security expert.

Kynan nods. "It's owned by Brad Murdock. Got the most up-to-date security, discreet staff on site, and the island is inaccessible on all sides except the north because of reefs."

Brad Murdock is a big time, A-list actor in Holly-wood. I don't know much about him but clearly, Joslyn has a good relationship with him since she thinks he'll let us use the place.

This has potential.

I turn to Barrett, who meets my gaze. "I need electricity to plug my laptop in. As long as it has that, I'm good."

Joslyn laughs. "It's a luxury estate. It has electricity, servants, and Wi-Fi."

"No Wi-Fi," I state, staring pointedly at Barrett. "You can't communicate with anyone on the outside. Nothing that can track back to us."

Her face falls as she realizes how isolated we're going to be. "But I need to be able to talk to my staff—"

"Sorry, Barrett," I murmur with a slow shake of my head. "We are going totally off-the-grid, okay?"

"But we'll be busting our ass on this end to find these people and shut them down," Kynan replies with confidence.

Barrett sets her fork down, not having touched a bite of her food. Giving a reluctant smile, she pushes up from her chair. "I understand. Now, if you'll excuse me, I'm not feeling all that hungry. I'm going to lie down."

I start to stand, but she waves me off. "Joslyn showed me your apartment. I'm going to go hang out there… be by myself for a while."

"Are you okay?" I ask, finding the odd mixture of worry and empathy swirling within me a bit disconcerting. I don't develop ties with my protection details. It muddles things.

Another thin smile. "I'm fine. Just tired."

We all watch in silence as she moves down the hallway before disappearing into my apartment.

"This has to be so hard on her," Joslyn murmurs.

"It will all be a distant memory soon enough," Saint offers, choosing to look on the bright side. "For now, at least she's safe."

Agreed. I force myself to start eating again, fighting against the need to check on her.

Pull her into my arms and comfort her.

Not part of the job description, yet I want to do it all the same.

CHAPTER 9

Cruce

I'T'S LATE BY the time I make it to my apartment. I need to get some sleep. After dinner, I'd checked on Barrett. I'd brought her a plate of lasagna and salad, but when I found her sleeping on the couch, I put it in the refrigerator for later. While I'm worried about the lack of food she's had today, if she's tired and needs to sleep, then that's what she should do. I've always been taught to listen to the body's needs.

There was no way I was going to leave her on the couch, so I went to my bedroom and pulled the bedding down to make room for her. Back in the living room, I was able to get her Chucks off without waking her up. She stirred slightly when I lifted her in my arms and carried her into the bedroom, but she didn't wake up until I laid her down.

"What's going on?" she'd murmured sleepily.

"Go back to sleep," I'd ordered softly.

She didn't question me, eyes sliding closed again. I watched her a moment, sure she was deeply under by the rhythmic rise and fall of her chest. She never felt me move a lock of hair off her forehead with my fingertips.

After I went back to the communal area, we worked on a plan late into the night. Joslyn contacted Brad Murdock, who was more than happy to give up his island for a matter of "national security". He wasn't told who was involved, and his staff will be told Barrett and I are nothing but filthy rich honeymooners with important connections. Their instructions will be to give us our privacy as much as possible and to tell no one we are there.

Saint worked his connections, so Barrett and I will fly via private charter to Virgin Gorda under fake names. From there, we'll take a boat to Marjorie Island, which was named after Brad's mother. Such private transportation will allow me to carry on weapons and other equipment—like an encrypted satellite phone and advanced security cameras.

I'm ready to call it a night, but I take a moment to peek my head into my bedroom. Barrett's still fast asleep, though at some point, she changed into sleep clothes. I can't see her bottoms, but she has on a comfortable-looking t-shirt. The clothes she'd been wearing are in a pile at the bottom of the bed.

As I exit, I leave the door open a few inches so I can hear her if she needs anything. I quietly move into the living room. These apartments are small, but they are beautifully appointed. The floors are hardwood with thick crown molding. It's furnished with masculine leather furniture that speaks to my tastes. Other than the master bedroom and bath, there's a living room, small kitchen, a guest room, and a half bath. I would sleep in the guest room—except I'm currently using it to store around thirty boxes I'd moved from D.C. a few months ago. I haven't had time to unpack them, and I don't feel like wrangling the dozen or so stacked on top of the bed.

The couch will do fine for tonight.

I pull a spare fleece blanket out of the coat closet by the door. After I strip down to my boxers and flop onto the couch, I pull the blanket over my lap. I don't want to give Barrett an eyeful if she gets up before me, but that's unlikely. I'm a light sleeper, and I rise early.

◆

IT'S A SOFT, hesitant cry, sounding slightly muffled. It still wakes me as if it were shouted in my ear, and I sit up, fully alert. I bolt off the couch, making my way swiftly to my bedroom.

I'd left the light on in the master bath, and I'm relieved to see that Barrett isn't under threat from anything except perhaps a nightmare. She's sitting up in the bed, covers pooled over her lap, one hand hovering at her chest.

"You okay?" I ask as I move into the room.

Barrett leans over, turns on the bedside lamp, and blinks at me slowly. Her voice is hoarse from sleep. "Yeah... sorry... didn't mean to wake you up."

"All good," I reply and since she's awake, I take the moment to offer her some food. "You hungry?"

"Weirdly, no," she answers with a slight grimace.

"You should try to eat something. I've got some canned soup I can heat up."

She shakes her head, grimacing again, which prompts me to ask, "Are you feeling okay?"

"Yeah," she exclaims with a falsely bright voice.

I cock an eyebrow. "Truth time."

"Truth is," she replies in a slightly quavering voice, "I could use some water. Would you mind?"

"Not at all," I say, then exit the room. My first stop is the couch to grab my jeans and put them on, since I'm pretty damn sure prancing around in boxers isn't overly professional. I head into the kitchen, grab a bottle of water from the fridge, and then return to the master bedroom.

Barrett fluffed the pillows against the headboard. She's propped against them, her legs stretched out under the covers. Her gaze is bold as I walk toward her, her eyes scanning my naked torso for a brief moment. She doesn't look away in embarrassment or chagrin, and it doesn't bother me in the slightest. I've never been averse to a beautiful woman checking me out.

I hand her the bottle of water. Without invitation, I take a seat on the edge of the bed, right at her hip.

I'm silent as she uncaps the water and takes a few small sips. Inadvertently, she rubs at her tummy as she does.

"Must have been a really bad dream," I say.

Barrett blinks in surprise. "What makes you say that?"

"You cried out in your sleep, and you're anxious right now," I point out with a casual shrug. "Not rocket science."

She doesn't reply, only takes another small sip of water.

"Want anything else? Some ginger ale, maybe?"

"I'm good," she assures me with pitiful smile. "But unfortunately, I'm wide awake now. Shouldn't have fallen asleep so early."

I watch her a moment, wondering just how much the stress of this situation is going to wear on her. "What was the dream about?"

Barrett doesn't answer right away. Picking at the label on the bottle, she meets my eyes and admits, "My mother."

It comes back to me in a flash. Her mother was killed in a home invasion when Barrett was just sixteen. She had just left to start her freshman year at MIT, so she wasn't there when it happened. Beyond that, I don't know any other details.

"It was weird," Barrett continues, speaking in a semi-flat voice as she recounts her dream. "It was like a combination of what happened to me yesterday and what happened to her."

"What *did* happen to her?" I ask softly. Ordinarily, I wouldn't push someone to relive a bad moment, but it seems she's struggling to make sense of things.

"She walked in on two burglars already in the house. It surprised them, and one of them shot her. They were caught and pled guilty. Young guys... early twenties. I don't think they ever intended to hurt anyone, yet they did all the same."

"That's senseless and tragic," I murmur, forcing my anger down.

"Yes, it is," she whispers. She gives a slight cough to clear her throat as she puts her water on the bedside table. Her voice comes out stronger when she says, "At any rate, in my dream, she was the one jogging down my street and I was in your position behind her. I saw the man turning to her... knew he was going to kidnap her. And I tried to reach for my gun... the way I know you did, but I didn't have one. I couldn't do anything to help her. I even tried to scream to warn her, but nothing came out. All I could do was watch as he grabbed her and pulled her into the back of the van, then it just sped off."

My chest squeezes tight, aching for Barrett. The

stress of her near kidnapping has clearly brought up old feelings of guilt and lack of control that she could do nothing to help her mother. She wasn't even there—thank God.

There's no thought in what I do. I just know she belongs in my arms, so I lean forward to pull her into a tight embrace. I've only known her a few days, yet because I saved her life yesterday, I feel I have the right to do this.

Because she trusted me with that story, I believe she thinks so, too.

Or maybe it's because I held her similar to this at the State dinner every time we danced, and it was obvious she liked it as much as I did.

Regardless, she easily sinks into me and presses her cheek to my bare chest. She doesn't even hesitate to wrap her arms around my waist as mine go around her upper back. I do nothing but hold her for several moments, and she lets me.

Eventually, Barrett shifts slightly and turns her head. Whether it's intentional or not—and I don't really give a fuck either way—her lips brush slightly across my chest before she tilts her head back.

Christ, she's beautiful. What started out as an embrace of empathy feels a little different right now. Like my skin is tingling where her lips touched my breastbone, and her soft curves feel lush pressed against my torso. Her mouth parts slightly and her eyes roam over my face, seemingly searching for something.

We stare at each other, and it feels almost dreamlike. It's easy to forget I'm her protector and she's a job for which I'll be well compensated.

Instead, all I see—all I feel—is a beautiful, vulnerable woman in my arms. I'm incredibly attracted to her, but in the past, I never would have let myself act on it.

Before I can even wonder if I should act on it, because perhaps I'm misreading the need I think I see in her gaze right now, Barrett surprises me by leaning into me, head tipped up so our mouths are just millimeters apart. With no control over my body, I dip my head closer to her.

Her breath wafts out, blowing across my mouth in a gentle caress, and I realize I'm at a dangerous crossroads.

I should drop her like a hot potato.

Back right off this damn bed, man.

But she fucking slays me when she whispers, "Kiss me, Cruce."

"Bad idea," I warn gently.

"Kiss me," she says again. This time, it's not a plea but an order. "Make me forget about things, even if just for a moment."

A moment?

Is she really that naïve?

Does she think all I would ever want is a moment

with my mouth on hers?

"Barrett," I mutter, forcing myself to pull slightly away.

Her eyes soften. Beg.

Fucking begs.

"Please," she whispers, one of her hands slipping behind my neck and putting pressure on it.

Urging me closer to her.

Fuck if I don't let her pull me, and then our mouths touch.

It's fucking electrifying, something I wasn't expecting. In every scenario I'd fantasized, I'd suspected kissing Barrett would be a slow melding. Instead, a bolt of lust surges through me and my eyes roll to the back of my head.

She gasps in surprise, and I know she feels it too. I know it because her hand grips the back of my neck hard, holding me to her.

Fuck me.

This has to stop, but... maybe we can let this go on for just a moment more. My head slants, her mouth opens farther, and my tongue invades. Barrett's fingers move into my hair, gripping hard and holding me tight. One of my hands moves to her lower back to press her tighter to me, and I don't spare a moment's guilt over the erection that's starting to occur.

Goddamn, it's an excellent fucking kiss, even if it is

so very wrong.

I pull back, my hands going to her shoulders to hold her away from me. Her chest is rising and falling, lips wet and swollen, and expression one of utter confusion.

"We can't," I say in explanation.

Confusion morphs to hurt, and that causes my chest to squeeze again.

I shake my head. "Barrett... it's not a good idea. I can't afford the distraction."

Hurt gives way to anger, and her eyes flash hot. "I am not a distraction."

"That's not what I meant," I growl, pulling her slightly closer to me with my hands at her shoulders. Leaning down, I put my face in front of hers. "I mean I can't get lost, and that fucking kiss right there made me want to sink down with you and never come up. I can't lose focus. My job is to protect you and nothing else."

Immediately, understanding dawns. Relief fills me when her face softens. She nods before lowering her gaze. "I get it. And I'm sorry I came on to you."

"It was mutual," I say, rushing to her defense.

Stubbornly, she tilts her chin up. "I started it by asking you to kiss me," she insists.

We stare at each other until she gives me a halfhearted smile. "It was a damn good kiss, though, right?"

"Words fail to describe it," I assure her.

Smile widening, she leans against the pillows and my

hands fall from her shoulders. My fingers want to continue to grasp onto her, but I reluctantly let go.

Slowly, I rise from the bed and take a much-needed step back. She avoids eye contact by reaching for the bottle of water.

"Can I get you anything else?" I ask.

She shakes her head, eyes darting to me a moment. "I'm good."

"Okay, then," I murmur, knowing I need to leave but not wanting to take that step.

Barrett takes a sip of water, re-caps the bottle, and sets it down. Her eyes lock with mine. This time, she stares boldly with a slight smile. "I'm good, Cruce. Thanks for checking up on me."

I give her a short nod and turn on my heel, leaving the room without looking back. Pulling the door behind me, I once again leave it open just a few inches in case she needs me.

CHAPTER 10

Barrett

I BUSY MYSELF with pulling the clothes out of my suitcase to repack it. Last night while searching for something to sleep in, I discovered Cruce's packing skills, well... frankly, they suck. He did nothing but toss everything in, smash it down, and zip it up.

I finally just dump it all out on the bed, carefully folding everything into segregated piles to make sure I have enough for our upcoming Caribbean "vacation". While my biggest fear would be that he forgot to pack underwear, I'm amused to find he emptied what has to be my entire lingerie drawer. There are over twenty matching sets of panties and bras, most lace and delicate silk. It's one of my guilty pleasures and sadly underutilized.

A knock sounds on the front door of Cruce's apartment, and I head through the living room to open it. It's unlocked and anyone could walk in, but I imagine manners supersede.

I smile when I find Joslyn standing there.

"Just doing a quick check to see if there's anything you need," Joslyn says as I step back to invite her in. "I can do a quick run out to the store."

"I don't think so," I say, having been through most of my clothes. Not like I needed anything dressy. The casual dresses, shorts, t-shirts, and jeans will work fine on a private island. "Are Cruce and Kynan still down with their... um... prisoner?"

When she nods, I turn for the bedroom to resume packing. Cruce said we'd be leaving before noon, which is fast approaching. Joslyn follows behind. Once we're inside, she casually starts helping me fold the remaining items.

"Sure brought a lot of lingerie..." Smirking, she gestures toward the stacked sets on the bed.

I roll my eyes. "That was Cruce. When he said we were leaving in a hurry, he meant it. He packed for me. As you can see, it's pretty easy to guess where his mind was."

"I imagine that's most men's minds," Joslyn replies with a laugh.

It makes me chuckle. "I get it. Time was of the essence, and he was in a rush."

Silently, she folds a t-shirt and places it on a similar stack. By the way she's chewing on her lip, I deduce she wants to say something, but it's obvious she isn't sure if she should tell me her thoughts.

"What is it?" I ask.

She shakes her head as if she's going to deny my curiosity, but I'm not having it. "Tell me."

Her shoulders lift as if she's unsure, but her gaze is direct. "I think there's something between you and Cruce."

Instinct says to *deny, deny, deny*, but I hesitate. Why lie? It's not like it's a big deal or like she's off base. There isn't anything I should be embarrassed about.

Besides, I'm not sure she's wrong.

"We had a moment last night," I admit, smoothing out a wrinkle in a shirt so I don't have to look at her. It may not be embarrassing, but...my belly still dips when I say, "Or rather... in the wee hours of the morning."

"Oh, do tell," she says, eyes wide with interest. She sits on the edge of the bed, laundry forgotten. "Because I was serious when I said I sensed something between you."

"We... um... well, we kissed."

"You kissed?" she exclaims loudly. Gleefully, she claps with clear delight.

"Yes," I murmur, hoping my lowered voice will encourage her to do the same.

"I knew it," she whispers fiercely. "I knew he was attracted to you, and I figured he'd make a move. Although, I imagine fraternizing with clients might be frowned upon in this line of work, but still... I'm all for the romance of it."

I shake my head, not willing to let Cruce take the blame—or credit. "He didn't make the move. I did."

She blinks a few times, mouth slackening in clear surprise. "Oh, well… nothing wrong with that."

"He put a stop to it," I continue. That same sinking feeling I felt in my gut when he gently pushed me away came rushing back. "Said he can't afford to lose focus while protecting me. The bottom-line conclusion Cruce came to—we can't do anything about our attraction."

"Well, I suppose an argument can be made for that. Like, maybe it's not the right time. Besides, nothing is more important than making sure you aren't kidnapped while ultimately catching the crazy people who are intent on doing so."

"Or maybe he's not really attracted to me at all, and he only used that as an excuse," I point out, zeroing in on what's truly bothering me.

"Now, that's simply not true," Joslyn says confidently. She stands, nabs a pair of yoga pants, then methodically starts to fold. "I'm telling you… I saw something on his face when he first brought you up here. It was a level of care that went above and beyond the expected worry about your safety. Trust me… I have good instincts when it comes to these things."

"Well, it doesn't really matter," I say, taking a stack of folded clothes and placing them in the suitcase. "Like he said, we've got more important things to worry about right now."

"Maybe it's something you two can resume when it's all over," she suggests, handing me a stack of t-shirts.

"Barrett," Cruce calls, his voice coming from the front door. It startles me so badly I jump, wondering if he's been inside the apartment listening to us. I didn't hear the door open.

"Back here," I force out, my voice squeaking. Joslyn furrows her brows, but I shake my head.

Cruce walks in… and why is it he seems a thousand times more attractive now that I know how he kisses?

Ugh.

"You about done?" he asks, raising an eyebrow at my suitcase.

"Yeah," I reply flatly, placing the last stack in and zipping the case up.

"Well, come on into the kitchen," he says as he pivots away from us. "Bebe's going to demonstrate how to work the satellite phone, and I want you to know how to do that."

Joslyn and I follow Cruce into the communal living area. Kynan, Saint, and Bebe surround the long kitchen counter. Bebe punches buttons on a rectangular phone.

When I come in, Saint gives me a slow once over. He grins, then gives an appreciative whistle. "Looking mighty beautiful this morning, Dr. Alexander."

I'm shocked by his brazen flirting. I look no different than I do any other day, except my hair is maybe a little tamer. Even though I feel my cheeks start to pinken, I flash him a return smile, lifting my chin a little. I hadn't realized how badly Cruce stopping that kiss last night had bruised my ego until Saint's obvious admiration washed over me.

I peek at Cruce, who is not even trying to hide the glare he has leveled on the other man. Saint pays no mind, grin only widening as he deliberately winks at me.

Cruce takes my hand, pulling me with him to the opposite side of the counter. It puts me opposite Bebe, so we'll have a good view of her demonstration. Cruce stands ridiculously close—our arms brushing every time either of us even minutely shifts—yet I can't find it in me to complain.

"Okay," Bebe says as she twists the satellite phone toward us so we can see the face. It looks surprisingly normal—only a bit thicker than a regular smartphone. Other than that, it's quite compact. It has a stubby antenna on top. The phone's surface has a small digital screen with four icons—*SOS*, *Messages*, *GPS*, and *Tracking*.

Bebe quickly but efficiently explains the phone's functions, making sure to stress the most important. *SOS*. "If you hit that button, we'll immediately send in a strike force hard and fast."

"And if we need to call someone, we just dial it like we would a regular number?" I ask.

Cruce answers my question by taking the phone, then punching in a number. When he hands it to me, I eye him questioningly.

He mimes for me to put it up to my ear, and I'm surprised when my uncle Jon's voice echoes through. "Cruce?" he says with worry.

"No, it's Barrett," I say as my eyes stay locked on Cruce. He's letting me say goodbye to my uncle before we leave for the island. I flash him a grateful smile. "We're just testing out the new satellite phone we're taking with us."

This morning, Cruce said my uncle had been notified about us going off-the-grid, but he hadn't been told where. He is not in the sacred loop—the sole members being the people in this kitchen.

"You're going to be just fine, Barrie," Uncle Jon says in a deep, gruff voice. "I have every faith Cruce will keep you safe while the rest of Jameson discovers who is behind this and puts a stop to it."

"I know," I reply, voice shaking slightly with emotion. While I'm confident Jameson will do their best by me, there's still a chance the lurking danger will end up crashing into my reality in more than an abstract way. That fact tends to sit at the forefront of my mind, especially since I lost my mom to a violent crime.

I'd be a fool to deny I'm a bit scared.

I *am* scared, and I'm going to let caution guide my actions. Following Cruce's orders quickly and to the tee will be my only priorities until they can find these guys.

As if he knows exactly what I need, Cruce presses his hand to my lower back as a means of support. Silently, his gesture tells me he has my back.

"It'll be just like a vacation," I tell my uncle with a short laugh, which comes off sounding fake and forced. He knows I don't do vacations, and that sitting around doing nothing will drive me crazy. I have to hold myself back from leaning into Cruce, wanting more than just the calming presence of his hand.

Uncle Jon snorts. "You relaxing is hilarious. But without the distractions you have at your office and lab—with nothing but time and quiet—I predict you're going to finish that formula in no time at all."

I sure hope he's right. The sooner I can get it done and into other people's hands—to where it's no longer a secret—the sooner I can return to my regular life.

"I'll do you proud," I assure him.

He's silent a moment before he says, "Honey... you've always done me proud. There's nothing more you need to do. Just stay safe and know your aunt and I love you very much."

"I love you both, too," I say, my voice choking.

Eyes concerned, Cruce pulls the phone from me. He

brings it to his ear, then says, "Sir… we're getting ready to leave. Kynan will keep you up to speed, but you won't be hearing directly from us until the threat has been neutralized."

I can't hear what my uncle says in return, but whatever it is, it's long winded. I imagine it might involve pleas to keep me safe or maybe even threats. He's the president of the United States and has power in his words, so it could be anything.

Whatever it is, Cruce gives a tight smile as he replies, "You have my word, sir."

And then he disconnects.

Bebe holds her hand out, and Cruce places the satellite phone in it. She puts it in a black, waterproof case, then holds up a small black box with a USB plug on the end. "This is a high speed, satellite Wi-Fi hotspot. It's encrypted but, as you all know, nothing is guaranteed."

"We'll only be using it if she finishes the formula, then we'll send it to multiple recipients for redundancy," Cruce says, placing it in the box. He turns to me. "Otherwise, we stay offline."

"But it's encrypted," I point out.

"We take no chances, Barrett. We're laying low, and you'll do what you can without access to the outside world. With luck, Kynan will figure out who this is, and we won't be there long, okay?"

"Okay," I answer reluctantly. While most of my

work comes from my own brain, I often need to look stuff up. I was able to download all the reference materials I might need to a hard drive, but something could come up that stumps me. If that's the case, then this could turn into a long, boring vacation.

Although, I can think of worse ways to spend down time than on a beautiful, private tropical island with a gorgeous man. And I wonder if Joslyn is right.

Is there something there?

After all this is over, should I look at it closer?

I've never had a meaningful relationship before. Nothing more than casual, meaningless sex.

I immediately dismiss that notion about Cruce.

The man is anything but casual and meaningless, but I can't tell if I'm observing him through a filter. Our meeting is anything but normal. We're getting ready to go on the run, and we'll be looking over our shoulders constantly. Under those circumstances, how can I even trust anything at all?

CHAPTER 11

Cruce

MARJORIE ISLAND IS just over four nautical miles northwest of Virgin Gorda, and it takes us only about fifteen minutes to make the trip by a boat Saint had waiting. We could have chartered someone to take us the short distance over water, but I don't like being trapped and Brad Murdock apparently isn't a boat man, so one isn't available at his private island.

I've got plenty of boating experience so it was the best choice to rent this twenty-five-foot May-Craft, which would also lessen the amount of people who would know exactly where we were heading.

Admittedly, I'm carrying a bit of tension as I wait for the Jameson team to find the root of all this trouble—that being the exact person or organization that wants Barrett. The longer it takes, the greater the chances said person or organization is going to make a better play for her.

The first grab-and-go plan was very unsophisticated. Whoever was behind it had no clue Barrett had private security protecting her.

But that doesn't mean this group is unsophisticated as a whole. It might only mean they tried the easiest plan possible. However, now they are aware she's being protected, they could easily come after her with more firepower, so to speak.

It's not unreasonable to expect this. Barrett's knowledge is worth a lot of money.

As in billions.

It stands to reason anyone determined enough to perpetrate a kidnapping that could result in untold riches would spend a great deal of money on a better plan to snatch her.

Which is another reason I'm glad I'm in charge of getting us from Virgin Gorda to Marjorie Island. By not chartering a boat, it ensures one less person who knows where we're going.

It's not fool proof, though. It would be nothing to bribe the pilot at the private Pittsburgh terminal we flew out of. He brought us first to Miami, where we re-fueled, then to Virgin Gorda. He had fake names for us, but I'm sure someone could offer him an amount of money that could prompt him to identify Barrett and me by the way we looked. Back in Virgin Gorda, plenty of people saw us getting on this boat, and there are only so many islands in the British Virgin Islands.

We can be found by determined people, and that's

why I can't let my guard down for a single second.

My anxiety is even more increased because of the woman sitting beside me as I navigate the blue waters. She's wearing jeans, a tank top, and a ball cap on her head. Her hair is in a ponytail while dark sunglasses hide her eyes. A pale effort to make it hard for people to identify her.

She's scared, and I know it.

Lost.

Out of place.

I want to give her more than protection. I want to reassure her. Take away her fears. Give her confidence this will all be over soon—that she'll be completely safe.

It would be my preference—so very weirdly—to give those things to her in the form of physical touch.

A hug, that's all.

Which is so fucking odd as I'm not a hugger. Plus, that's also way too dangerous because a hug can lead to a kiss.

Another punch-to-the-gut kiss that will electrify me. Fry my fucking brains out like it did last night.

Christ, how the hell am I supposed to be in close confines with her? Complete seclusion, actually.

How can I do that and control myself around her? Especially now, when I know without a doubt, how easily she came into my arms and begged me to kiss her that she wants the same thing?

So goddamn unprofessional, Cruce. Get a fucking hold of yourself.

Marjorie Island looms closer, and I study it critically as far as how easy it would be to breech. The island is smallish, but it has two prominent hills that rise up significantly from the beach. The main house is built on top of the tallest one. I've been told it's only seven acres total, which doesn't sound like a lot until I think about having to patrol it, but I'd still take it over Pittsburgh. I've been told the back side of the island is surrounded by shallows and reefs, making it too dangerous to approach by boat, so that helps at least.

The sprawling one-story main house faces toward Virgin Gorda. It's surrounded by trees and lush greenery and I'm sure somewhere in all that vegetation is a path leading upward from the beach. There are a few smaller buildings off to the western side, which I assume is for staff and perhaps maintenance. I can't see them, but supposedly there are three small guesthouses on the eastern side.

For our stay, we'll be in the main house, which was necessary for our cover. We're supposed to be rich, well-connected honeymooners who want the entire island to ourselves.

More importantly, the main house is on the most elevated part of the island. It has three hundred-and-sixty-degree views, so we can see if anything or anyone is coming our way. Luckily, if it's by boat, they'd have to come straight at us by taking the same path I'm on now as I start to throttle down as the dock comes into view. In the cover of darkness, an extremely determined person could breach security by parachuting in or anchoring a boat and swimming to shore. Good thing two of the bags we brought are full of equipment Bebe put together, including trip wires and thermal-imaging cameras. One of the first things I'll take care of is a satellite call back to Bebe so she can walk me through the security setup.

As I cut speed, letting the boat coast, I take in the two men on the dock. They're expected—the island's manager and a staff person to help move all the bags. I'm okay with this, but only because the specialty equipment and weapons are in locked and padded duffels that won't arouse any suspicion. But I'm also going to make sure I boot them and anyone else still on the island as quickly as possible.

Both men are dark skinned, wearing crisp, pressed khaki pants and tropical shirts in reds, yellows, and oranges. The younger one steps forward, then takes the rope I toss him to tie off the boat to the dock. When it's secure and I cut the engine, I let Barrett precede me off. The young man takes her hand and helps her across onto the wooden boards. I hop up next to her.

The other man—older by about twenty years—is holding a small, round tray with two coconut drinks bearing festive umbrellas.

"Welcome to Marjorie Island, Mr. and Mrs. Belton," he says in a lilting Caribbean accent as he offers the tray. "I'm the manager, Samuel. This young man is my son, Thomas."

I take a coconut drink and hand it to Barrett, then grab the other. Because we're honeymooners, I put my arm around her waist and pull her in close to my side as I smile at the man and his son.

Barrett, knowing we have to play the part of an in love and recently married couple, slides her arm around my waist in return before saying, "Thank you. We're so excited to be here."

Samuel nods, tucking the tray under his arm. "Now, if you'll follow me… I'll take you up to the main house and show you around. Thomas will bring up all your luggage."

"You were told we wanted absolute privacy, correct?" I ask.

Eyes flashing with amusement, he grins broadly. "Of course. We'll be leaving as soon as we get you settled in."

"And just how will you be leaving?" I ask curiously.

"My other son, William, will swing by and get us. He's a fisherman. In fact, he's more than willing to drop off any fresh catches to you any day you wish. You only need to let me know."

"That's very kind." Barrett flashes a smile.

"But we'll most likely catch plenty of our own fish, honey," I say pointedly, giving her a squeeze.

Samuel tips his head back and laughs, waving a playful finger. "I understand completely, Mr. Belton. You want privacy on your honeymoon. For this, I cannot fault you."

With a wink at the man, I motion at Barrett with the hand holding the coconut cocktail. "I mean, look at this woman... Can you blame me?"

I want to laugh when I see Barrett blush, because she should know this is necessary banter for our ruse. Yet, it's clear she's affected all the same. Of course, I wasn't lying about my appreciation of her looks. She's a stunning woman, so it only made sense to point it out.

Barrett curves her body into mine, then slaps me playfully on the chest, deciding to add her own flare. "Baby... stop. You're embarrassing me."

Chuckling, I lean down—being completely spontaneous and a little self-serving—to give her a quick but soft kiss on the mouth. When she almost jerks away from me in surprise, I hold her tighter in warning.

As I return my attention to Samuel, I see him watching us with twinkling eyes, clearly a romantic at heart.

"Let's head up to the house," he slyly suggests. "Get you settled so we can get out of your hair."

He glances at his son, who is carefully pulling out each bag and setting them gently on the dock. "You have this under control, Thomas?"

"Yes, sir," he replies in the same carefree accent.

Barrett and I follow Samuel onto a covered winding path that leads up to the main house. The trees and foliage are so dense it provides almost complete shade as we traverse the walkway lined by tropical bushes laden with fragrant flowers.

The path comes out into a small open courtyard with a wide porch. The house was built with a dark wood, but it has so many large, un-paned windows and an open design, which will allow a clear view through to the rear of the house and the blue waters on the other side of the island.

We follow Samuel in, and Barrett gasps over the opulent beauty. Gleaming blond wooden floors—probably maple—and plush teak furniture with over-stuffed linen cushions first catch my eye. When I spot a rectangular gas firepit in the room's center, I feel my brow crinkle as I wonder why anyone would want to start a fire in the tropics.

Samuel points to the walls along the perimeter, which are basically framed floor-to-ceiling glass. "All the walls slide to open to the outside. I highly recommend opening them in the morning and evening hours as the breeze is spectacular."

We follow him around a corner into a huge kitchen of chrome and glass. "The refrigerator and pantries are well stocked. The phone on the counter reaches me directly. I can bring you groceries as often as you need."

Glancing at Barrett, I see her slowly taking it all in with wide eyes and a gaping mouth, her expression portraying this might be the most wondrous place she's ever seen.

Traversing up a short staircase, we follow Samuel into another wing. The master bedroom dominates, and it's a wonder for sure. It's massive with a four-poster king-sized bed smack in the center, which is covered with mosquito netting.

To the right is the master bath, but there are no walls closing it off. An open shower and tub are on a slightly raised dais with a beautiful double vanity along the wall. There's a small door, which I assume is the water closet.

Astonishingly, there's an indoor pool inside the huge bedroom. It's probably only fifteen-feet wide, but it's long, rectangular, and leads directly onto the balcony under the glass-paneled wall.

Samuel walks over to the glass wall that leads onto a patio. When he presses a button, the wall starts sliding panel by panel into recessed pockets until it completely disappears.

"Oh, wow," Barrett murmurs.

It's obvious Samuel takes immense pride in this feature. "Visitors to Marjorie Island tend to spend a great deal of time in this room."

"I imagine so," she replies as she wanders onto the balcony. It's furnished with a beautiful set of furniture and another gas fire pit.

"Mr. Murdock said you will be staying here for an extended period," Samuel says.

"A few weeks." I keep the answer purposefully vague.

"Well, we normally send someone in daily to clean, change the linens, and replace the towels. Would you like that?"

"Actually," I reply hesitantly, eyes on Barrett as she leans onto the balcony railing and admires the blue waters. "I think we'll be just fine on our own."

"Of course, sir," he replies with a half bow. "But like I said… I'm a phone call away if you need anything."

"Thank you, Samuel," I reply just as Thomas comes in with the first armful of our luggage.

It takes another twenty minutes for Samuel to show us around and Thomas to unload the boat. I tip them each a hundred, for which they're extremely grateful. My hope is the generosity will translate into discretion. When we were in the kitchen, I'd checked out the food supplies and pantry. We easily have enough to keep us well fed for a few weeks.

I walk with the men to the docks, leaving Barrett to the lunch she insisted on making. The three of us make small talk until Samuel's other son comes to pick them up. After they leave, I give the boat a once over, making sure it's secure before heading back up to the main house.

Barrett put together a salad with what looks to be grilled chicken. She certainly didn't have time to cook it, so when Samuel said the provisions were well stocked, he hadn't been kidding.

It's quiet as we eat, and I have no clue what Barrett's thinking. My mind is on getting the security equipment set up before the sun goes down.

So, it startles me when she says, "You should take the master suite."

Furrowing my brow, I lift my head. "Excuse me?"

"The master suite. I mean… you're the one doing all the hard work of protecting me and stuff. You should have that bedroom."

I put my fork down, then cross my arms on the table. "Actually… we need to stay in the same room."

"We do?" she asks, pulling her chin toward her chest in surprise.

"For safety," I say bluntly. "While the chances of anyone finding us or making it past the security alarms without alerting me are slim, I want you in the same room with me at night while I'm sleeping."

"Oh," she mutters, eyes on her salad.

"I'll sleep on the floor," I say.

"Sure," she replies vaguely, picking through her salad with her fork. But then she jerks her head up. "I mean…

no. You can't sleep on that hard floor. The bed is huge, and we're both adults. We can share."

"I don't know if that's a good idea," I drawl.

She cocks an eyebrow. "Why? Am I unsafe with you or something?"

"Of course not," I snap, offended she'd even suggest such a thing.

"Then what's the big deal?" she mocks, batting her lashes.

Jaw locked, I stare. I have to loosen it to grit out, "No big deal."

Except sleeping in a bed with you all night will be about the most torturous thing imaginable.

But I keep that admission to myself.

CHAPTER 12

Barrett

THERE'S NO DISORIENTATION as I wake up. I immediately know I'm on a private island in the Caribbean in a luxurious home owned by a famous movie star, currently being hunted by people who want to kidnap me, and pressed against a half-naked, well-muscled, and gorgeous man.

Shit.

How did I end up plastered against Cruce's side? It took significant effort throughout the night to cling to my side of the huge bed. It's been the same for the last three nights.

Each night, I'm exhausted at bedtime. I've pretty much been working the same long days I did back in the States, and I was ready—actually aching—for sleep when I tumbled onto the mattress. Cruce doesn't go to bed at the same time I do, which has made it less awkward for sure. I've been able to drift off fairly quickly.

But thereafter, things weren't quite that easy. I had a terrible time staying asleep, nightmares and needing to pee constantly waking me. Each time I woke, sometimes sitting up in the bed or quietly rolling out to use the bathroom, Cruce woke, too.

"You okay?" he'd ask.

Each time, I replied, "Yeah… gotta pee."

I'm pretty sure he thinks I have a bladder problem at this point, but each time I returned to the bed, I lay on my side, back to him, with my fingers curled into the sheets on the edge of the mattress for anchoring.

Each time before I fell back asleep, I gave myself a stern lecture to stay on my side of the bed and not to inadvertently roll his way.

A lot of good that's done because the sun is now up, and my worst nightmare has come to fruition. I'm snuggled right up against Cruce.

He's on his back, and my face is pressed into his upper arm. I've got one arm curled under me, supporting my head, and the other resting on his belly.

Oh man… right on that part of his stomach at his navel where a sexy line of hair starts, running down into the cut-off sweatpants he's wearing. I peek at the expanse of exposed skin before me as he's bare chested.

Damn it!

I can hear seagulls screaming outside as we left the glass panels open last night. This was done only after Cruce determined it would be impossible for anyone to scale the outside of the house and enter as the outdoor balcony was built outward over free air space.

Casting my eyes down to where my hand rests on him, I can't believe I'm touching him so intimately. The urge to move just a few inches forward until I can touch that trail of hair is strong. My fingers literally cramp as I restrain myself. Against all my wants and desires, I very slowly lift my hand off his body.

"About time you woke up," Cruce murmurs and my hand freezes, hovering just over his stomach.

I scramble away, putting a good foot of space in between us. "I am so sorry," I squeak as I stare with wide eyes. "I did that in my sleep. It wasn't intentional, I promise."

Lazily, he rolls his head on the pillow to give me a sly smile, those blue eyes sparkling. "It wasn't a hardship, Barrett."

God, why did he have to make that sound so sexy?

"Regardless," I reply almost primly, "I'm sorry for encroaching."

Cruce just stares. He's obviously contemplating something, I can tell. I brace, wondering if he'll take the time to remind me why nothing can occur between us. Or perhaps he'll gently let me down by telling me he's gay, which we both know isn't true, but it would be the gentlemanly way of letting me know he's not attracted to me.

Instead, he rolls on his side, props his head on one

hand, and presses the other into the mattress. It brings us shockingly close again. Instinctively, I scoot back another few inches, mainly so I don't assault him with my morning breath.

"Do you know you talk in your sleep?" he asks.

I blink in surprise. I did not know this, but it's been a long damn time since I've slept with a man all night. No one around to point anything like that out.

"What do I talk about?" My tone is hesitant… fearful it will be something embarrassing.

"Interesting stuff," is all he says, not even trying to hide the smirk spreading across his handsome face. "Lots of little sounds, too."

Searching my memory, I try to grasp onto any fragments of my dreams last night. I don't remember anything sexy that would cause me to moan, but then again… I don't remember half the shit that woke me.

"Are you messing with me?" I ask, hoping beyond hope that's the case. If not, I'm going to die from mortal embarrassment. Right now.

He ignores my question, which is intentionally evil on his part. "I'm starved. Eggs and bacon sound good for breakfast?"

Cruce doesn't wait for my answer. Instead, he flashes a charming grin and rolls out of bed. I lock my eyes onto his body, because it's impossible not to when it's so damn gorgeous. Plus, I cannot miss the hard-on he has.

It presses right up against his cut-off sweatpants, tenting them in the middle. I only get a brief glance before he's striding out of the bedroom.

Rolling to my back, I let out a huff of frustration.

Damn it... I want Cruce.

And he clearly wants me.

Unless he was dreaming about Scarlett Johannsen or something.

But what if that erection was because of and in reaction to me?

I don't consider myself an aggressive female when it comes to the opposite sex. I've never been the lead in making something happen, mostly because of my inexperience but I've also not been shy about it if the perfect opportunity presented itself either.

In fact, I suspect there might be something wrong with me because I'm sitting here analyzing my sex life with the same detached, scientific curiosity with which I handle my work. That right there says I'm not all that great at this sort of stuff.

As such, I need to let this go and let it go for good. Cruce and I have more important, pressing matters to worry about. I need to concentrate on my work, and I can't make things awkward for Cruce.

I vow to myself I won't think about Cruce in an untoward fashion again, hoping to God I have the willpower to honor that promise.

♦

OUR FIRST FULL day here, I'd decided to claim the dining room table as my office. It's huge—seats sixteen—and runs perpendicular to one of the glassed walls that look out over the front of the island. I can see the dock with the boat we rented, the white beach to the left of it, and in between those points and the main house, the canopy of trees and bushes that hug the small island hills.

I'm having a tough time concentrating, and I pin that on a few things. First and foremost, this isn't my office and lab. There's no familiarity here. Granted, anything my eyes land on is stunningly beautiful—from the interior of the house out to the blue Caribbean waters—but none of that means anything when I'm trying to concentrate on my groundbreaking work.

I'm also distracted by the fact that, at any moment, some military strike force could come barreling up to the beach in an armored boat, shoot Cruce dead, and kidnap me. No one has said it yet, but I suspect my refusal to discuss my research is going to cause me pain at some point.

I'm guessing torture is what is in store for me, and that alone has my stomach constantly knotting up.

And then, there's the man walking the length of the beach while checking the trip wires. He does that about ten times a day. Prior to checking the equipment, he navigates the entire perimeter of the island, making sure all alarms are operational. This has become his routine, and I expect he is bored out of his mind.

I move my gaze away from Cruce back to my laptop. I'm reading an old article written during the eighties by a Russian physicist. Many of my peers won't go that far back in their research, thinking anything more than twenty years is too outdated. But I find compelling kernels of information that will cause a new idea to fire in my head enough to make the effort worth it.

I make a few notes on a yellow pad beside me, tapping my pencil against my chin. I never write in ink because, more often than not, the minute I jot an idea down, I'll erase it and write something more expansive and infinitely more intelligent. It's the way I process.

When I'm done for the evening, Cruce will have me lock my laptop and notes away into a secure, steel vault located in, of all places, a guest bathroom in the east wing of the house. I guess if someone wanted to steal valuables, it would be one of the last places someone would think to look.

I concentrate on the article, getting lost in the words and jotting notes. When the front door opens, I lift my head, sliding my attention that way. Cruce walks in, looking like he's totally settled into island life. He's wearing swim trunks, a light blue t-shirt that does amazing things to his eyes, and tennis shoes.

Wait... the tennis shoes won't work.

"You need flip-flops," I point out as he starts my way.

"Yeah... not really all that mobile in flip-flops," he counters, snagging an apple out of a bowl on the kitchen island. He takes a bite, his white teeth flashing a moment before he chews.

"Island all secure?" I ask, pushing my chair away from the table and stretching my back.

"As secure as I can make it," he says, coming to a stop right beside me. He bends, peers at my notes, and reads my last line aloud, *"It sucks not having Wi-Fi."*

Lifting his head, he grins. "Those are some ground-breaking thoughts, Dr. Alexander."

I shrug. "What can I say... I'm a modern girl. I don't like being cut off from the world."

"Well, modern girl," he drawls, pointing a finger around the apple he's holding. "You've been working at this table for seven straight hours today. The last three days, you didn't take a break. You even ate your lunch here. So, I think you should take a break to keep your body healthy and alleviate my boredom."

My back *is* sore, since the comfort factor of these chairs suck. Sure, they're gorgeous, designer, and feel great on the ass for the length of a meal, but they weren't made to be sat in all day. Rolling my shoulders, I groan at how tight they are.

Without thought, Cruce sets the apple down and moves behind me. He places his large hands on my shoulders, then starts to massage them.

I groan again, this time in discomfort as he hits knot upon knot, but also with relief because I can feel them releasing.

"Okay," he says, hands moving from my shoulders and going under my armpits. He hauls me out of the chair, then gives me a tiny push toward the hall that leads to the master suite. "That's it. Go get a bathing suit on. You're going to take a half-hour break—at a minimum—and we're going down to the beach. I'll give your entire back a massage, then you can lay on a towel and watch me fish for our dinner. How's that sound?"

"Like heaven," I admit as I face him. "And usually a luxury I never let myself have."

"Why do you work so hard?" he asks, his head tilted in curiosity. "I mean… I get putting in a fifty- or-sixty-hour workweek to anyone who's dedicated, but you work anywhere from ninety to a hundred. Why?"

My brow furrows. "Because I love what I do. I get immersed. Lose track of time. Isn't that why anyone spends so much time doing certain things?"

"No," he replies firmly with a slightly sad note. "Most people don't do what they love. They watch the clock, and they can't wait to stop for the day. They dread going in to work in the mornings. You're lucky, Barrett, to do what you love."

"Do you love what you do?" she asks.

"Well, I did when I was with the Secret Service," he says, then his smile turns sly and calculated. "This job is a little too new for sure, but I can't say spending the afternoon on the beach with a beautiful woman in a bikini is a horrible job perk."

Laughing, I give him a mock, chiding glare. Then I sober instantly as I realize something. "Sorry... no bikinis. In fact, no bathing suits. Your packing job was shitty, and you didn't bother to pack me one damn bathing suit."

"I could call Samuel to ask him to bring some over," he replies thoughtfully, but then I see a metaphorical light bulb go off over his head. "Or rather, just wear one of those fancy lingerie sets I threw in there. God knows you had enough of them. They're no more revealing than a bikini would be."

I stare, my jaw dropping slightly. Some of them are way more revealing, as in the lace and silk are extremely see-through.

But some aren't.

Some would work. He's quite right they have as much—or rather just as little—cloth covering the important parts.

Besides... I'm on an isolated island, running from kidnappers and dependent on this man to protect me.

I've already developed a level of trust with him that I've not had with most people in my life. I don't think I'd feel a lick of insecurity or awkwardness in wearing my underwear in front of him.

Funny what having someone save my life and continue to protect it can do in that regard.

"Okay," I say with a wink before turning on my heel. "Bra and panties it is, but only half an hour on the beach. Then I'm coming back in to work some more."

"Don't forget sunscreen," he calls. "There's some in the bathroom."

"Got it," I say without breaking stride. "But you'll have to do my back for me."

I swear, I think I actually hear him groan in response.

CHAPTER 13

Cruce

I'M NOT EXACTLY sure when the semi-nerdy scientist started looking not so nerdy anymore. I imagine it was the evening I'd escorted her to the president's state dinner.

But right here and right now—as Barrett walks back into the living area—is the moment she goes from semi-nerdy scientist to the sexiest woman in the entire world.

She chose a baby-blue matching bra and panties in a satin material. Her breasts are fantastic... heavy and testing the strength of the straps. The satin is thick enough to shield her skin, but not so much it can hide her nipples popping against the material.

Those fucking panties, which cut high on her hips and low on her flat belly, have me dying to know just how much of her ass is going to be shown. I know it's going to be as beautiful as her front view.

No, I wasn't thinking straight when I packed for Barrett. I just threw as much shit in the suitcase as I could. Yes, I'd known I was pulling handfuls of stuff out of her lingerie drawer without really paying attention to it.

And no... I didn't know she'd need a swimsuit. Had no clue we'd be hiding out on a tropical island.

But as I watch her saunter my way, I'm thankful as fuck I didn't grab a bathing suit or two and that Barrett apparently has an appreciation for fine lingerie. Also, incredibly grateful she doesn't seem to be shy.

It's only after I focus on Barrett's face that I realize my eyes spent a little too much time on her body parts. Her cheeks are flushed, her arms coming almost protectively over her stomach as if she's trying to hide from me.

I play it off, giving a dismissive wave. "See... not much different from a bathing suit."

Without waiting for her to reply, I pivot toward the door, snagging two beach towels I'd gotten out of the linen closet while she was changing. I open the front door, motioning for her to precede me out.

She does, and I follow.

Big mistake... because I almost trip a few times since I'm not watching the cobbled stone path as much as I should as we descend toward the beach. That's because my eyes are pinned to her ass, much of which is not covered by the thin blue satin.

And weirdly... the thing that makes her the sexiest—the most attractive to my senses—is she still comes off as the nerdy scientist. Maybe it's because her hair has been pulled back in a rough ponytail since this morning, pins holding her bangs out of her way while she bent over her laptop.

Or maybe it's the way she sometimes talks to herself, low and under her breath, about formulas and hypotheses. Or better yet, the corny, scientific jokes she makes and snorts over that I don't get at all.

Or perhaps it's the total package. More brilliant than most people on this planet, the body of a goddess, the face of an angel, and a certain amount of dorkiness to round it all out.

Whatever it is, I'm coming to the realization I'm not sure I'm going to be able to handle this.

Protect her? Fuck yes… got that covered.

Being in her presence, alone, with no good reason why I shouldn't kiss her?

That's becoming more difficult to fight against.

This morning, waking up with her snuggled into my side—her hand innocently resting on my stomach—was an instant fucking hard-on. I'd laid there trying to get myself under control for I don't know how many minutes, but all I could think about—fantasize, really—was that I wanted to roll over on top of her, spread those pretty legs, and drive in deep.

Yeah… might be one of the most difficult things I've ever been faced with.

Barrett Alexander.

"Your eyes are on my ass, aren't they?" Barrett's voice penetrates my thoughts, and I stumble again.

I right myself, guiltily lowering my gaze down to the path so I can walk straight, but I mutter an admission, "Just a man, Barrett. Not a saint."

She snorts in reply, so I defiantly look at her ass again, the whole way down.

The beach area is a swath of silky, fine, white sand that runs about thirty yards from the dock, curving inward to make a tiny, shallow cay. It's set up with several Adirondack-style chaise lounges with large yellow umbrellas to provide shade if wanted. At the end of the sandy beach, there are a line of flowering bushes that lead into more trees and vines, giving way to a thick jungle of native plants. Earlier this morning, I'd pushed my way through it armed with a machete I'd found in the maintenance building to navigate the exterior of the island.

I walk over to one of the chaise loungers, then lower the top half so it lies flat. Placing one of the beach towels over it, I ignore the umbrella beside it. Barrett needs some sun, which is good for the soul.

"On your stomach," I order.

She doesn't hesitate. First, though, she holds out a can of spray sunscreen. I hadn't noticed it before, but why would I have?

"I already did my front," she says before turning away.

Her knee goes to the chaise, palms to the top, and she lowers herself down. Barrett turns her head, stretches out, then nestles her hands under her cheek.

For a moment, I let my gaze swing out across the blue water. I scan the horizon where I can make out the hazy outline of Virgin Gorda. No boats in the water near us. Nothing in the sky.

No threats at the moment.

Taking a deep breath, I focus on the gorgeous woman before me. Bending, I use a hand to shield her face and start to spray her shoulders and back. I have no clue if she managed to get any part of her backside, but I liberally shower the exposed parts of her ass and legs.

When I'm done, I push the can under the chaise to shield it from the hot sun.

"You want that massage I promised?" I ask, hesitant to actually touch her body without explicit permission.

"Mmm," she replies lazily, her eyes closed against the brightness of the late afternoon sun.

I take that as a yes, but I don't have any intention of doing anything other than relieving her muscle tightness. Her upper back and shoulders have to be a mess based on the long hours hunched over a computer.

"Scoot a little," I murmur as I sit on the edge of the wide wooden platform near her hip.

Barrett complies, and I twist at the hip, placing my hands on her skin. It's already warmed by the sun. The spray is oily but not thick, making it easy to glide my hands over her. A few light strokes before I start digging my fingers and thumbs into her muscles, eliciting groans from her. I don't go heavy with my pressure because she's a delicate woman. I don't want to bruise her.

But I do try to make my moves therapeutic, concentrating on her shoulders for the time being.

I try not to think about other parts of her body I'd like to stroke. Because it's way too easy for my mind to go there when my hands are on her, I strike up a conversation.

"You a beach person?" I ask.

She shrugs, never once opening her eyes as I continue to massage her. "I'm not sure. I've not been enough to really know. My mom tended to take me on educational vacations… like a week touring the Smithsonian or something like that."

"So, no Disney vacations, huh?" I ask.

Barrett chuckles. "Honestly, it's not somewhere I ever wanted to go. I was happy going to the Smithsonian or hitting up art museums in New York. Stuff like that."

I don't say anything because I find it a little sad. Kids should want to go to Disney, right?

"Well, you don't know what you're missing," I say, moving to her mid-back. I don't hesitate to push my fingers under her bra strap to massage the muscles there. After giving the water a quick scan, I move my gaze back to her skin. "Disney is the best place on earth."

Barrett laughs. "Pardon my skepticism seeing as that recommendation comes from a bad ass, former Secret Service agent who is now a private mercenary."

"First," I reply in an over-exaggeratedly offended tone. "I'm not a mercenary. I'm a paid protector."

"Semantics," she replies.

I ignore her. "Second, you imply my love of Disney somehow lessens my masculinity, and those are just fighting words. In fact, when this is all over, I'm dragging you there and taking you on Mission Space at Epcot. When you're screaming and crying like a little girl and hanging onto my manly muscles because of your fears, I'm going to demand an apology."

The full-bellied laugh I get from Barrett makes me smile, but it dies all too swiftly. "So, you went on a lot of vacations like that growing up?"

"Yeah," I reply, a fond smile on my face. "My dad played poker with his cop buddies on Thursday nights, and he was really good. His winnings let us go on vacations like that every year."

"Where else would you go?"

I scoot down the chair a bit, so I can move to her lower back. "We'd do stuff like travel to national parks or rent a cottage at a beach. One year, Dad made enough to take us to London for a week."

"That sounds nice," she admits, her eyes finally opening. "Your whole family seems nice."

It's not the first time we've talked about our families. We've spent a lot of time filling voids over the last several days—usually at meals—by casual talk. Family is always an easy topic.

Or, at least, mine is.

Barrett is a little thinner on happy family memories as her parents were taken away from her. By the time President Alexander took over her guardianship, she was already leading an "adult" life at MIT, despite only being sixteen. She'd had to grow up way too soon.

I withdraw my hands, having given adequate attention to her muscles. Anything more would just be to satisfy my desire to touch her. "Want to get in the water for a bit?"

"Sure," she replies lazily as she starts to push up.

But then I hear a vague "thwapping" sound, and I snap my gaze outward over the water. Way in the distance, I see a helicopter flying this way.

I'm not too alarmed as there are choppers that fly out of Virgin Gorda daily to do scenic tours for tourists. I saw two this morning.

But I'd rather be safe than sorry when I can, so instead, I take her by the hand and pull her up. Nabbing the towels and the sunscreen, I pull her backward toward the path that leads to the house, far enough up the foliage completely shields us.

We wait, hand in hand. Within a few minutes, the helicopter zooms right over us. I can't see any details, just a flash of it through the leaves, but it flies by without any decrease in speed.

"Is that necessary?" Barrett asks, her head tipped up and her eyes heavy with worry.

"Just don't want to take any chances," I tell her.

Her mouth draws downward, and she shakes her head with despondency. "I thought I'd be able to forget all this stuff for just a few minutes."

Fuck, that gets me. I don't think twice, because apparently when Barrett feels heartache, the best thing I know how to do is wrap her in my arms.

She comes easily, letting me wrap her in an embrace, and I give her a reassuring squeeze. "It's not forever. You can do this. You're strong and brave."

"You don't know I'm brave," she murmurs.

I pull away, glancing down. She refuses to meet my eyes, so I call her name. "Barrett."

Finally, she tips her head back.

"From the beginning, you've been brave about all of this. Never complaining. Pushing forward with your research with focus and determination. Hell, you watched me shoot a guy. When he fell at your feet, you didn't even freak out. So yeah... you're one of the bravest women I know."

I get a wan smile. For her effort, I take her by the hand again. "Come on. Let's go play in the water a bit."

Smile brightening, she lets me lead her to the sand, back into the bright sun. Right up to the warm water's edge. When we step in, she doesn't let go of my hand.

I don't let go of hers, either.

CHAPTER 14

Cruce

LEANING MY FOREARMS on the wooden rail, I look out over the water. It's a super bright and sunny day, bringing Virgin Gorda into focus a bit more. I've already done my morning perimeter check of the island, and I've been hanging out on the balcony that runs the width of the front part of the house.

The satellite phone rings, and I pull it from my pocket. It's only the second time Kynan has called in the last five days we've been here. The first was just to make sure we were all settled in and to see if there was anything we needed.

No clue why he's calling now.

"What's up?" I ask as I connect the call, glancing over my shoulder into the open glass wall. Barrett sits at the dining room table, so engrossed in her work she doesn't even react over the phone ringing.

"How are things going?" he asks.

"Good. Same. All secure."

"That's good," he replies, but I can hear the anxiety

in his voice. "Listen… we're going to go ahead and send a team after the arms dealers. Keith Spire is tapped out. He doesn't know anything, so we're turning him over to the police. President Alexander is arranging it."

"Any luck on finding the arms dealers?" I ask, my eyes scanning the water.

"Yeah… still in Oman, which is weird. We haven't had time to set up a workplace there or anything, but we think it's best we just go in quick and hard. I'm sending in August, Sal, Benji, and Kara."

He doesn't need to explain what he means by "quick and hard". I can read between the lines. Most likely, they're going to take these guys into a rural area and do some hardcore "encouragement" tactics to get them to talk. I've read that a water-boarding plank can be set up in the back of a work van, allowing your torture to go mobile.

Details like that should turn my stomach, but I can't seem to care what they need to do to get more information.

"I expect it's going to take a few days to get there, set up some recon, then make the plan to snatch them," he explains, so as to keep my expectations in check. "But hopefully once we get them, we can get some quick information."

No holding in my slight sigh of frustration. "Okay, man… thanks for the update. I'll let Barrett know."

"Sure you two don't need anything?" he asks again.

"We're good. Just keep us updated."

"Okay. Later, bro."

"Later."

I disconnect the call, then put the phone back in my pocket. Turning toward the house, I study Barrett. She's bent over her laptop, hands scrunched in her hair, while she reads something on her screen. I let my gaze move over to the whiteboard she often writes on. It's crammed with frenzied scribbles I think might be formulas.

She works so fucking hard she completely tunes out the rest of the world. If I weren't here to make her eat, drink, and take bathroom breaks once in a blue moon, she'd perish.

Shoring up my resolve, I leave the balcony, stepping into the dining room. She doesn't acknowledge me, probably hasn't even noticed I'm here.

"Time to take a break," I say as I walk down the length of the table.

Barrett doesn't even hear me. When I reach her chair, I stick my arm out and wave my hand between her face and the laptop.

She jumps, then looks up with a dopey smile. "Sorry... guess I was zoned out, huh?"

Chuckling, I reply, "Zoned in, more like it. When you get involved in your work, I genuinely believe the world could burn down around you and you wouldn't even notice."

"I'm sure that's an exaggeration." She sniffs primly, but then tilts her head in curiosity. "What's up? You never interrupt my work."

"Kynan just called. They're sending a team after the arms dealers who are still in Oman."

"The man who tried to kidnap me still isn't talking?"

I shake my head. "I think they're pretty convinced he doesn't really know anything. At any rate, they're turning him over to the cops."

Barrett's gaze slides off to stare blankly at the wall. Her voice is flat when she says, "So we're going to be stuck here a while, right?"

"Probably," I say, then I take her upper arm and force her to stand from her chair. "Which is why, every afternoon—right around this time each day—you are going to take a break. You work at that table for too long, and it's not good for you. I demand at least half an hour, but I'd be happier if you committed to at least an hour break."

"Cruce," she whines, trying to flop back down in the chair. "I can't. I'm getting close to something."

"And you'll continue getting closer after your break," I say staunchly, bending to physically pick her up in my arms. Pivoting, I carry her straight to the master suite. Once inside, I set her down.

"Now, go put on your finest set of panties that will

pass as a bathing suit, and let's go."

"I don't want to just go lay on the beach. That's not relaxing to me when I want to work."

"Which is why we're taking the boat out and doing some snorkeling," I cut in, enjoying the way her mouth snaps shut. I nod toward the dresser, where we'd unpacked all of our clothing. "Now… get changed."

◆

BARRETT CLIMBS OUT of the water in her raspberry-colored bra and panties. I'm not about to tell her the material is now slightly transparent. I can't help scanning her body, but I quickly avert my eyes as I help her back into the boat.

It turns out the woman who spent her vacations in museums as a child has a serious case of snorkel love. I had to make her get out of the water as the sun was starting to set because I wanted to head back around the island soon.

We hadn't gone far on our adventure, just to the other side of the island where I couldn't get within a few hundred yards of the shore because of the reefs, but the snorkeling there was fantastic. I lost track of the amount of times Barrett grinned at me around her snorkel.

Now, she flops onto one of the cabin seats at the rear of the boat. She removes her mask first, then her fins. I do the same before pulling out a couple of bottles of water from a cooler I'd packed, handing one over to her.

Grinning, she settles against the cushion. "That was freaking awesome."

"Glad you enjoyed it," I murmur, holding my bottle of water up to her in a silent toast.

"Can we come back out tomorrow?" she asks with excitement.

"I told you... you're getting up from that table to take a break every damn day, so if you want to snorkel each day, that works for me."

"The colors down there are so vibrant and amazing," she murmurs with a slightly disbelieving shake of her head.

"Australia," I say. "You need to snorkel there. Their reefs are amazing."

"Consider it now officially on my bucket list," she replies with a laugh. Pausing and seeming to consider something, she then starts laughing harder.

"What's so funny?" I ask.

"It's just... I really don't have a bucket list. That was my first item really."

"All work and no play makes Barrett not have a bucket list," I croon with a chuckle.

"I need one, though," she says with contemplation, her smile slipping a little. "I guess if there's one thing this little adventure has taught me it's there's a lot to life I've been missing out on."

I nod, throwing her a little sage advice despite the fact she hasn't asked for any. "Don't lead your life with regrets. Don't wake up one day and say, 'I wish I would have'."

She nods solemnly. "Yeah... if I were to die tomorrow, I think I'd have some."

"Like?" I prompt.

She gives me a halfhearted shrug as she glances down at her bottle a moment, before giving me her pretty eyes. "I guess one would be not having enough fun. Not having a childhood. Not having friends. It's been school and work and nothing else. Just this little bit of forced time away from my office has been a bit of an eye opener."

"I can imagine," I say in agreement, happy she's realizing something important about herself.

"What about you?" she asks. I blink in surprise, not sure exactly what her question is about.

"What about me what?"

"Regrets," she says, lifting her chin. "If you were to die tomorrow, would you have any major regrets?"

"Too many to list out," I say with a light laugh, but when I see how solemnly she's studying me, I know she's not asking about petty or incidental things. Coughing, I clear my throat, one thing coming to mind.

Something I've never told another living soul.

But right now, having this honest conversation with

Barrett, I want to bare it to her.

"When I shot the man who tried to kill your uncle," I say, letting my words hang in the air.

She nods in understanding as to who I'm talking about.

"A part of me regrets it," I admit.

Face blanching, her eyebrows shoot sky high before she shakes her head in denial. "No. You were a hero. You saved Uncle Jon's life."

"Yeah... get that part," I murmur, staring out across the water. When I give her my attention again, I say, "But as time has passed and I've reflected on it, I think I regret taking the kill shot. Perhaps I could have shot him somewhere else. Disabled him, maybe."

"No," Barrett firmly says. "No. You can't second guess, and that's all it is... second guessing. That's not regret."

"It is," I state, refusing to back down. "I regret not giving that guy a chance to live."

She takes in my words and the seriousness of my tone before she nods in acquiescence. Tilting her head, Barrett asks, "Is it awful? Feeling that?"

I shake my head with a smile. "Not too awful. I had just a fraction of a second to react. There were no good choices. I saved a life. So, I can regret what I did in hindsight, but it's not torturing me or anything. I don't let it weigh me down."

"That's good," she says with a relieved smile. "Because you're such a good man. You don't deserve to have that bearing down on you. I know I'm eternally grateful for what you did, and I don't have a moment's sympathy for that man. He deserved what was done to him."

"Probably," I agree. "But you asked about regret, and there you have it. And for the record, Dr. Alexander, I've never shared that with anyone before. In fact, Kynan specifically asked me about it when he interviewed me and I out and out lied to his face about it. So, it's our little secret, yeah?"

"Yeah." She grins. "Our secret. I'll take it to the grave."

CHAPTER 15

Barrett

I LOVE IT when I'm in the middle of a good dream and the details are bright, the sensations are hyped, and I'm so deep under there's no danger of awakening. Perhaps I've thought so much about how I woke up day before yesterday, with my body against Cruce's and my hand on his stomach, that it led me to dream about the same thing.

Maybe it was the time we've been spending together. We floated in salty, clear blue water, talking about life and happenstance. When he would take a moment to scan the horizon, I was sneaking glances at his perfect chest and arms. Cruce didn't try to be surreptitious. He just stared, not being gross but also not hiding his appreciation.

It could even have been last night, enjoying a quiet dinner on the outdoor balcony as we watched the sun set into the water. Cruce asked me about my research and the work I had left to do on my formula. He let me talk for over half an hour about it. I could tell he didn't understand a damn thing I said, yet he was engaged and interested. While he couldn't help me on the scientific side, he had plenty of direct encouragement to give me.

Whatever the reason, I'm now currently dreaming of being pressed against Cruce's body again in one of the best dreams ever, and I'm not going to let it go. He smells so good, and his skin is warm. My hand flattens, touching as much of his belly as I can, then I rub my cheek on his shoulder.

I go still when Cruce shifts, and my heart starts beating so fast it feels like my chest might explode. But then I remember… dream.

I can act with impunity.

My lips curve upward in a sly smile that only I know is on my face. I slide my hand south, letting my fingers finally touch those crisp dark hairs known as a happy trail. They certainly make me happy as I follow them to the edge of the waistband of his cutoff sweats.

I frown, sad my dream isn't more tailor made for me. Because he should have been completely naked in my dream, so I wouldn't have to mess with clothing.

But whatever…

I dip my fingers under the waistband, immediately met with warm, silky skin stretched over what feels like granite.

I encircle his impressively sized shaft—dreams totally rock—and grip him without thought because it's my dream and for me alone. He's so thick my fingers can't even wrap completely around him, and I give a hard squeeze.

When Cruce groans loudly, my smile goes wider. I give a stroke, all the way to the tip, and rub my thumb across the wetness there before gliding back down.

"Christ," he mutters, and the words sound like he's being tortured.

I jolt and snatch my hand away, forgetting all about taking what I want in my dream.

But then his large hand clasps onto my wrist, and he growls, "Don't."

And well… that feels way too real. The way he's squeezing, the slight pain in my bones and his words seem to be louder and excruciatingly clear to my senses. Not a foggy dream at all.

My eyes pop open. Slowly, I tip my head up.

That's when I realize I'm not dreaming at all. In fact, I'm not sure I ever had been.

Cruce's face is harsh in the morning light. I can't tell if he's just irritated or angry.

"I'm sorry," I mumble, earnestly trying to pull my hand back.

Holding tightly, he speaks through gritted teeth. "Don't," he says again. When he adds, "Stop," I almost don't believe my ears.

Don't. Stop.

My eyes widen at the implication. Before I can even hazard what it all means, he's pushing my hand back down. My breath becomes nonexistent when he releases me, only to lift his hips and push his sweats down enough to release himself.

Once again, he grips my wrist, shoves it to his erection, and practically snarls, "Take it."

I don't need provocation, orders, or begging from him. Rolling, I shift up onto my elbow and take his cock in my free hand. He groans, lets his head flop to the pillow, and squeezes his eyes shut in what I'm hoping is full surrender.

My gaze slides down his body, which is lightly tanned from his time in the sun these last few days, and to the beauty straining against my hand. I start stroking, slowly at first, but then faster because I like drawing forth the wonderful variety of grunts and hissing sounds he makes. His hips thrust counter to my movements, his breathing ragged.

In my entire sexual life to date, I've never brought a man to completion this way. I've never been with someone satisfied by only that. They've either run out of patience and climbed on top, eager to thrust out an orgasm, or pushed my head into their lap.

Which... either is fine. I like both, but something about Cruce letting me do this to him—the most basic of sexual gratification—seems to imply his gratefulness for what little I'm offering.

He has no clue I'd offer him anything, but I'll enjoy him exactly how I have him in this moment.

On an upstroke, I squeeze a little harder than usual.

Cruce hisses, "Fuck yes, Barrett. Just like that."

So, I give it to him, just like that.

I jack him hard and fast, dragging my gaze from what I'm doing up to his face. It's beautiful in the way it's pinched and strained—as if he's trying to hold off his orgasm, yet he's desperately seeking it at the same time.

"Come for me, Cruce," I murmur, and he snaps his eyes to mine. "Give it to me."

"Fuck," he barks as his back arches. Groaning, he starts to ejaculate all over my hand and his stomach. I stroke him through it, watching the milky white strands erupt as he moans out his release.

And damn... I may not have come, but I feel so fucking satisfied right now.

Cruce lets out a harsh breath as he lowers his hips to the mattress. I gently slide my hand up his still-hard length, then up so I can run my fingertips through the wetness on his stomach.

Should I cuddle with him? Put my head on his shoulder? Can I stroke his chest without him reading too much into the intimacy?

Should I say something? Like what? *Thank you, that was awesome?*

I have no chance to ponder these questions—well, insecurities—because Cruce rolls my way so fast I let out a yip of surprise. His mouth crashes down onto mine with a possessive ferocity I didn't think should be possible after he just had a very satisfactory moment that's still wet between us. Yet, he seems starved to claim me.

The kiss is so vastly different than the one we shared in his small apartment at the Jameson headquarters. That one was born of security and comfort.

Only one word comes to mind with this one— *domination.*

I roll to my back, submit, and let him take whatever he wants from my mouth. His tongue invades, laying total waste to me. Before I can even think to reciprocate, it's gone.

His mouth is at my breasts now. Somehow, he has my sleep shirt hiked up to my throat. His teeth and tongue work at my nipples, and my hips shoot off the bed in response. Cruce's large hand goes to my stomach, presses me down into the mattress, then shoves his hand into my sleep shorts.

Right into my panties.

Finger right into my...

"Cruce," I call in surprise as he thrusts in deep, only to pull his finger out to drag it over my clit.

And then... his hand is gone, and I want to cry.

But he's not gone. In fact, he's shifting in the bed to kneel at my hips, dragging my shorts and panties right off me. Cool ocean breeze from our open wall hits me, and I'm barely cognizant Cruce is now shoving my legs apart, pressing his face right into me. His beard is both prickly and soft against my thighs.

His tongue shoves in deep and hot, and I've never, ever experienced that before. I don't ever want to experience anything else again. Just want to stay right here like this, which is why I grip tightly to his thick hair.

I try to pull him harder into me, but it's impossible as his tongue is in impossibly deep.

But then it's gone. I don't even have time to cry out my frustration before his tongue lands on my clit. He works it hard.

Fast.

Jack hammering me with it, in between long, slow sucks.

It's the best feeling I've ever felt, which is probably why my orgasm comes out of nowhere. It shreds me head to toe and inside out until I'm not sure there's a single molecule left that will ever be the same.

"Oh God," I moan, cry, rant, shriek... all at the same time.

Cruce chuckles and groans, which shoots more pleasurable sparks through his mouth into me and I swear I come again.

Softer this time, but it still feels so freaking good.

He gives me one final lick. A long one... straight up my center. It makes my toes curl, then he's moving right up my body. He drags his lips along my skin, the wetness around the edges of his mouth and beard leaving a trail that feels surprisingly dirty-good.

Then his mouth returns to mine, and I taste a combination of us mingled together. I groan in satisfaction as I wrap my arms tightly around his neck, and our kiss is now a combination of our first time. Secure, sweet, but still possessive in a way that says this isn't a onetime only situation.

Cruce wants more, and I'm going to give it to him whenever he wants it.

His mouth eventually lifts from mine. He rolls to my side, briefly burying his face in my neck for a moment. He gives a slight groan of recrimination before lifting his head.

"I'm sorry," I blurt out. "I really thought I was dreaming. Or... maybe I even was to start out, but I didn't mean—"

"That chicken's already flown the coop," he murmurs, his eyes softening a bit.

"No crying over spilled milk?" I inquire. Perhaps he also thinks about the white semen that was splashed all over his stomach earlier, because we start to snicker simultaneously. I move right into him, not caring if this is too cuddly or intimate, and I wrap my arm around his waist. "I'm really sorry. I crossed a line you didn't want to."

"It's fine," he murmurs. Putting his arm around me, he gives me a return squeeze of reassurance.

"That was more than fine," I point out.

"It was fucking great, and we both know it," he mutters. "Going to get even better when I recharge."

Relief flushes through me, indicating I might have been assuming it really was a onetime only thing.

Definitely making it clear I would have been devastated had he declared it so.

"Would you like me to make us some breakfast?" I ask.

Another chuckle from Cruce, and he squeezes me again. "Not going to take that long for me to recharge."

Pleasure hits me between the legs, indicating it's not going to take me that long to recharge either.

CHAPTER 16

Cruce

IT'S DIFFICULT FOR me to occupy the time on this island. Barrett spends her days with her face pressed against her laptop or scribbling in a notebook. She's feeling hamstrung out here in isolation, cut off from her research assistants and the other scientists in the community she can reach out to for some brain picking. Relying only on herself—her brains, her intuition, and her imagination—she's becoming frustrated over the lack of progress she's making.

I'm frustrated waiting on something to happen with the situation. The team Kynan sent just made it to Oman today, and they are in the middle of active reconnaissance of the two arms dealers. That will take a few days at least. Barrett and I being able to return to a normal life will most likely hinge on what they find out.

For now, though, everyone agrees Barrett and I should stay put for the time being.

We've only been here eight days total, but it seems like a lot longer. I spend the daylight hours patrolling the perimeter while Barrett works, scanning the horizon for any hint of danger, and sometimes fishing in the small cay for our dinner.

It's now my sworn duty to pull her away from her work in the afternoon as I'd promised, because she needs the break so she doesn't run herself into the ground. She's more dedicated than ever to finishing this formula because she knows it could also be our ticket to freedom. So, I make her go down to the beach or snorkeling, just for a little while to refresh her mind.

At night, though, I'm a selfish fuck because I make her come to bed at a decent hour. It's not because I think she needs more of a breather, or that a fresher mind might be gained with better rest, but because of no other reason than I want to be inside of her.

Her hand on my cock two mornings ago opened the dam, and I have a never-ending stream of need for her that can't seem to be fully quenched. So, after we finish dinner and clean the kitchen, I do a final perimeter check of the island while she tries to squeeze in another hour of work.

Then I return to the main house, and I actually drag her away. Sometimes, she begs me to let her finish a thought or a note. Sometimes, I even give in.

For the most part, though, I don't.

I just sweep her off to wherever I want to have her to start the evening, knowing we'll end up in the big bed in the master suite.

She created a monster—made me submit to something I never should have let happen—and now she has to live with the beast she awakened.

Barrett isn't complaining, though. If anything, she always ends up begging because even though we started off this sexual relationship with a quick, hard jacking where I let her have control of me, it's not the way we've rolled since.

I like to lead.

I like to get her frenzied and out of control, to where she'd let me do anything I want.

Foreplay... I fucking love it. There's not a part of her body I haven't touched and claimed in the last two and a half days.

The sun is starting to get heavy, dropping nearer to the horizon. I check my watch, confirming it's getting close to the time to head up to the main house and make us dinner. I've taken over all the meals, not because I'm a better cook—I'm not—but mainly to give Barrett those extra precious minutes to work.

Like I said... when night falls, she's mine. She doesn't belong to the future of free energy for those hours.

I've already completed my last perimeter sweep. Not surprisingly, all infra-reds and trip wires are perfectly set up. The weather has been good, and no one has been on the island except Barrett and me.

We are running low on a few things, though. I'll need to call Samuel to see if he'll make a quick supply run out to us. I'll meet him on the docks as I don't want to run the risk of him seeing any of the cameras or wire strung strategically in areas that look most approachable up to the main house.

This morning, I took some steaks out of the freezer to thaw. I'm planning to do them on the grill with some potatoes. We've had fish every night since we've been here—fresh caught and delicious—but I want some damn beef.

Making my way up the path, I eyeball the trip wires I placed through the foliage in case any potential intruder decided to try to sneak up off the path, which are covered by the infra-red cameras. By the time I hit the front door, I've gone out of hyper-vigilant, single-purposed protector mode and into *can't wait to spend time with Barrett while I protect her* mode.

I hate myself for feeling this way. I've put my own feelings and desires over what's best for Barrett, which would be to put one thousand percent of my energy into watching over her. It means I shouldn't let her distract me, and I shouldn't lose myself in her.

In essence, I'm letting her down in the long run.

I'm letting Kynan down.

If he knew I was fucking her, he'd kill me, then fire

me.

And yet, not going to stop. What's done is done, and now I've had her, I'm just going to have to risk my fucking job because I'm not going backward.

Barrett isn't just some lay.

She's not a hookup. Not a one-night stand.

She fucking means something to me, and that's probably why it's the best damn sex of my life.

I'm goddamned smitten with the woman I'm protecting, and I have no business being in this line of work if I can't keep this shit separated.

When all this is said and done, Kynan deserves my resignation and he'll get it.

I hurry into the front door and through the foyer, immediately zeroing in on Barrett at the large dining room table. Clearly hearing me enter, she sits straighter in the chair, flips her laptop closed, and looks over her shoulder with an expression I can't quite pinpoint the meaning of.

It's a mixture of what might be excitement and regret.

"What have you done?" I tease.

Face flushing, she pushes out of her chair, hands clasped in front of her chest as she turns to face me fully. "I think I might have had a breakthrough. No, not *a* breakthrough. *The* breakthrough."

When I cock a brow in question, she squeals before

running to jump into my arms. I catch her on instinct, but even if I hadn't, it wouldn't have mattered since she wraps her legs tightly around my waist and laces her fingers together at the nape of my neck, clinging like a monkey. She sits just slightly higher, so she has to tilt her head down. Shamelessly, I cup my hands around her ass to support her position.

"I think I did it," she exclaims, practically vibrating with energy. "I'll have to um… go back over it again, but I really think I did it."

"As in you can release it to the world?" I ask.

"As in I can release it to my employer, who will then turn it over to the United States, but yes… I think my work is done. Like I said… I'll need a few hours tomorrow to double check some things, but this could be it."

"Fuck, Barrett," I mutter, then smack a hand to the back of her head so I can pull her in for a rough, congratulatory kiss. It's swift and brutal, but her gasp of pleasure assures me she likes it.

When I pull back, I stare into her eyes. "I'm so proud of you."

"So, we can go home, right?" she asks, again with excitement brimming in her eyes, but I also get an undercurrent of ruefulness. Maybe she's sad to be leaving our little paradise, and I can't say I relish the thought either. I haven't had a chance to try to figure out what the future could hold for us in the real world.

"I'm not sure," I reply hesitantly as I lower her to the ground. Bringing a palm to her cheek, I bend to peer at her. "I need to call Kynan, and he'll have to discuss everything with your employer and uncle. They might feel it needs tested first—"

"But that could take weeks," she exclaims in frustration. "I thought once I gave my work away, once I put it out into the world, the danger would be over."

"Probably," I say. "Let me put a call into Kynan first, and we'll—"

She cuts me off by stepping into my body, putting her hands behind my neck and pulling me down for a kiss that says *shut the fuck up for now*.

When we kiss, it's full of congratulations, pride, and a little bit of sadness that most likely our time in paradise is coming to an end.

When she pulls away, I take a moment to let my eyes roam over her face. Her hair, which is a complete nerdy mess. The slight swelling to her lips from that kiss. "Hungry? I was going to grill some steaks."

"Yes, I'm hungry," she replies softly, hands going to the button on my cargo shorts. "But not for food right now."

Just those words. The way her fingers fumble as she tries to get inside my pants. The sexy seductress mixed with the clumsy scientist. For whatever reason, the combination turns me the fuck on.

Barrett is *the* one for me.

My dick is almost fully hard by the time she shoves my shorts down and frees it. Her hands are feather soft as they stroke me. I kiss her again, let her play with me for a bit before I reciprocate with my fingers. She's wet and throbbing in no time at all, but the same could be said for me.

I could carry her off to our bed. It's been well used these last several days.

But instead, I spin her toward the dining room table, breaking our kiss only to bend her over it. She gasps as I hike up the tiny cotton skirt she's wearing, sucking in a deep breath when I drag her panties all the way down. When I tap an impatient hand against one of her ankles, she dutifully lifts to let me pull one leg free. I leave the silk dangling from the other ankle as I straighten.

God, she's fucking gorgeous from behind. Her naked ass. The slight peek of her pussy as I shove her legs farther apart with my own. All perfect.

Moving in close behind her, I line myself up and drive in deep. Barret groans, her hands clawing at the mahogany wood as I fuck her. I've got a hand on her hip, one on her shoulder to hold her in place, and I thrust hard.

Over and over again into the woman I think is *the* one.

I give her all I've got while taking exactly what I need. When I feel her pussy starting to tighten around me, I'm not the slightest bit surprised when my body reacts accordingly. She's coming... therefore, I simply must come, too.

I slam in deep, hold there, and lose myself completely.

CHAPTER 17

Barrett

"**I** FEEL GUILTY," I tell Cruce as my feet swing back and forth. "Just… doing nothing."

We're sitting side by side on the end of the dock. Despite Cruce's best efforts to get me to walk around naked, I'm dressed, but scantily so. I'm wearing my laciest, most miniscule bra and panty set in a translucent white lace. I might as well be naked.

Dressed in nothing but shorts, Cruce holds a fishing pole. We're waiting to hear back from Kynan on what the game plan is. Because I essentially have no more work to do on my formula, I did not say no to a late morning on the dock to soak up some vitamin D in the form of sunlight.

I feel guilty for other reasons, which I cannot divulge to Cruce. He'd kill me, and I'm still not sure they wouldn't cause total panic within him over my transgressions.

Yesterday, I did something Cruce, Kynan, and Bebe had hammered into me *not* to do before we left.

169

Stay offline, they had said.

For my safety.

For Cruce's safety.

But I'd made my breakthrough yesterday afternoon. While Cruce was out walking the island and doing his duty to protect me from the bad guys, I suddenly had one of those moments of clarity where not only did a light bulb go off, but I also felt like the scientific heavens had opened up and poured divine light down onto me.

I'd realized the elements that had been missing to get the lighter atomic nuclei to combine to the heavier nucleus, thus creating the beautiful process of nuclear fusion.

Of course, it's all theoretical and I was calling on a dusty memory I had of something I'd read in an old periodical I did not have digital access to.

So, my guilt comes from the fact I could not resist the temptation to confirm what I was ninety-nine percent sure about, and I logged onto the satellite Wi-Fi Bebe had given Cruce to use only in an emergency.

To try make myself feel better, I justified that everything was encrypted and protected by the powers of Bebe, but since she'd been the most vocal in explaining there's nothing in the digital world that's absolutely safe and foolproof, I knew I was taking a risk.

I'd emailed my research assistant, taking no more than probably thirty seconds to do so. I immediately logged off after stating I needed the response as soon as possible.

I waited an hour, logged back on, and saw his response. It confirmed exactly what I needed to know.

I started to log back off, eager to return to work and do some theoretical hole punching to test the validity of my findings. But then one last thought occurred to me, and I let my excitement over the fact the end might be near get the better of me.

I sent a quick email to my uncle. Keeping it short, I'd been offline within mere seconds.

Dear Uncle Jon,

I'm close. Really close. Love you and thank you for all your support. See you soon.

Barrie

Yeah, I feel guilty as hell about sneaking to do those things. I'm suffering extreme remorse. However, I have to look at the positive. I woke up this morning, re-testing all my theories by working in reverse order. I did it four times until I realized... there was nothing else I could do. It had to go to testing.

Cruce had called Kynan and gave him the news. We were both told to sit tight and be patient while Kynan figured out the next steps as it could take a few days. He wanted to talk with my lab to figure out how to transfer my data securely from the island to their servers. He also intends to talk to my uncle to see if he has any other safety concerns. As Kynan pointed out to Cruce, my formula being finished doesn't mean I'm safe. Even if others take my work and start actual reactor testing, it still doesn't mean someone won't want to pick my brain apart.

Right now, we are in the safest spot possible—although Cruce hypothesized it was probably going to be safe to go home soon, after adding some modified protection at my home.

Makes me sad this is all going to be over.

My time here with Cruce, I mean.

We've been here almost a week and a half. While stress has been high, and we've been socially isolated, I have to say some of my happiest moments ever have been here. Granted, it's the nights or the early morning hours when I'm in his arms or he's inside of me. It's the conversations we share over meals. The way he moves. How he looks at me.

It's how my body reacts to him. How sometimes when I just look at him while I'm up in the main house working and he's on the beach, standing guard, I get almost giddy with emotion.

I don't want this to be over. Yet, I don't know what awaits us back in the normal world.

"Have you ever just sat around and done nothing?" Cruce asks, jolting me out of my reverie. He reels in his line, pulls it all the way out of the water, then sits the pole on the dock beside him.

"Huh?"

"You said you feel guilty," he reminds me, compounding said guilt not only for sitting here doing nothing, but also for disobeying the rules that were put in place to keep me safe. "Have you never truly just relaxed?"

Putting my hands on the dock slightly behind me, I lean back, lifting my face to the sun for a moment. I tip my head to the right, settling my gaze on him before I answer.

He's so handsome. So good and attentive and sexy and genuine. I owe my life to him, as well as all the ways in which I've changed over our time together.

Slowly, I shake my head. "No. I've never just done this, and I need to thank you."

"Why?" he asks as he rolls to lay fully on the deck.

I follow suit, sliding my hand over to find his and turning my face back to the sun as I close my eyes against the brightness. Our fingers link. "Thank you for making me see the pleasure in just laying here on a hot wooden dock on a sunny day while doing nothing. Thank you for making me slow down sometimes."

He rubs his thumb over the back of my hand. "Promise me you'll continue to do this back in the real world."

"Won't be as fun without you," I reply, internally wincing when I realize saying that may be way too forward.

Too clingy? Needy? Girlie? Desperate?

His hand jumps in mine slightly before he locks onto me with a tight squeeze. It's enough to make me turn my head, the hard wood of the dock hurting my skull, as I open my eyes.

He stares straight at me. "Wouldn't want to deprive you of fun."

Hope swells within me, and my lips curve upward. "Really?"

Cruce gives a careless shrug. "I mean... you're all right to hang out with."

I pull my hand free of his, only to use it to pop him in the stomach. He curls up, grabbing onto his stomach, and looks pained. Smiling, I only roll my eyes. I hadn't hit him hard.

Grinning, he leans over and puts a palm on the nape of my neck, pulling me up into a sitting position. His mouth touches mine, and I can't help but sigh into the kiss.

If feels so damn right.

I feel like I belong to him.

It's hard... ignoring the twinge of guilt over not telling him what I did by getting online contrary to specific orders. But that was almost twenty-four hours ago, and nothing bad has happened. I was online for no more than two minutes total, if that.

It seems like everything is working out to achieve my dreams. My bonus is Cruce. I've made something with him that he wants to continue to explore.

The kiss deepens. I bring my hand to his wrist, locking on tight to hold him there forever.

"Can we make a deal?" he asks, practically groaning the question into my mouth.

"Mmm?"

"You never wear bathing suits again when we're at the beach or poolside together. Just lingerie. And the more see-through the better."

Giggling, I pull away from him slightly. His eyes are sparkling in the sun as he grins. "I am not dressing like this in public."

"Then maybe I'll just keep you on a private island all the time," he suggests.

"I could get on board with that," I muse, bringing my finger to my lips and coyly peeking up at him.

"Could you get on board with me taking that little white lacy number off you right now?" he asks, his voice rumbling with desire. Gaze dropping to my chest, he skims his finger along the edge of the lace cup, sending shivers up my spine.

"What if a tour helicopter flies over?" I ask.

"I'm in the 'don't give a fuck phase' of this idea," he

replies gruffly, his hand now moving to the clasp at the front to unhook it.

Wantonly arching my back, I push my breasts up and out, giving him access to do whatever he wants.

Just before he unsnaps my bra, the satellite phone on the dock next to us rings.

Cruce groans, dropping his forehead to mine for a second, before he sighs and rolls away from me. He reaches out, nabs the phone, and taps the button to connect it. Pushing another to put it on speakerphone, he puts it between us.

We've been waiting for this call from Kynan to tell us what our fate is. Can we come home or are we stuck out here until some testing can be done?

"Kynan," Cruce says as he answers. "Got you on speaker. Barrett is here with me."

"Well, I've got some good news and some bad news," he replies.

Figures.

Cruce gives me an encouraging smile. Somehow, I don't think he'd mind being stuck here for a bit longer. After that kiss we just shared, not sure I would either.

"We think it's okay to bring you two home," Kynan continues. "Although the president wants to talk to his security advisors as he's worried about the continued threat to Barrett. He's organizing that now."

Cruce and I exchange a longer, more meaningful

look. Kynan has no clue we've just committed to continuing to see each other. That we're not having an awful time right now. But we can't stay here forever. We both have lives we need to get back to.

"I'll have something definitive for you tomorrow," Kynan promises. "My gut instinct is it will be information on a private charter out of Virgin Gorda. I'd start getting your bags packed."

"All right, man," Cruce replies, his tone businesslike. "We'll hang tight until we talk to you tomorrow."

"Later," Kynan mutters, and the call is disconnected with one sharp tone emitted.

Cruce sets the phone down, wincing apologetically. "I know that's probably not what you wanted to hear."

"On the contrary," I reply silkily, wondering if I can pull off the inner seductress within me. I move my hand slowly to the hook Cruce had been so close to touching, and I give it a practiced flick. It pops open, and my breasts spring free. I don't even have a moment's embarrassment. By the look on Cruce's face right now, I actually want to roar in triumph.

"You present a tempting offer, Dr. Alexander," he murmurs, his eyes pinned on my chest. He's so adorably sexy when he calls me that, or maybe it's truly just the expression on his face as if he just found water after a long crawl through the desert.

"It's all yours for the taking," I assure him.

He reaches a hand out slowly, then grazes the back of it across one of my nipples. It shrinks, hardens, and stands at attention. "So responsive to me," he says as if he's never been more awed in his life.

Staring, he doesn't make a move, as if he wants to hold on to this small moment of simple appreciation.

"Cruce," I murmur to get his attention.

It takes a moment for his eyes to slide to up to meet mine, but when they do, I have his undivided attention.

"I've never had this before," I say, motioning between us. "This level of intimacy with a man, I mean."

He nods, solemnness filling his eyes. "Same. This is new territory for me."

"Is it real?" I ask. "Or do you think it's because of the circumstances we've been thrust into?"

Cruce peers over the water for a moment. I don't take it as a means to be evasive. Merely a way to perhaps focus his thoughts.

When his attention returns, it's with a clarity I recognize. It's the same expression he had on his face when he shot the man who was going to kidnap me. I can only assume it was the same when he saved my uncle's life.

Determination.

Acceptance of an apparent truth.

"It's real," he says. "As real as it can get between two people."

CHAPTER 18

Barrett

THE MINUTE CRUCE'S hand covers my mouth, I instantly come awake. His other goes to my shoulder where he gives a gentle yet urgent-feeling squeeze. It's dark and there's just a small amount of moonlight filtering into the room through the open glass wall.

His voice is low, barely a whisper, but I can hear something within it that makes my blood run cold. "Someone is on the property. The infra-reds have been tripped. I want you to get quietly out of bed and get your shoes on."

His meaning is clear. We're going to make a run for it, and there isn't time for anything but shoes. I'm only wearing one of his t-shirts. I don't even have on panties. He has on nothing but a pair of boxers. It has to be serious if he's willing to take flight like that.

Cruce's hand slides off my mouth, and he takes half a second to press a hard kiss on my lips, which reassures me a little. Then I follow his orders, quickly rolling out of the bed. We meet at the closet, silently putting on our tennis shoes in the moonlight.

It's as he's reaching for his holster, which has a loaded gun within, that the bedroom door flies open. I can't help the scream that comes from my mouth, but it's cut short by Cruce pushing my chest hard and sending me back into the closet. I'm blinded by a flash of white light, an explosion rattling me so hard I fall to my knees.

I immediately try to take stock of injuries, but I don't hurt anywhere other than my ringing ears. I'm still blinded, so I assume it's Cruce pulling me to feet. I'm so dizzy I start to sink again, feeling suddenly nauseous.

Then I'm tossed up and over his shoulder. He takes off at a run out of the bedroom. Muffled sounds of what I think might be people shouting at each other tries to pierce through my panic. As I blink furiously, my vision starts to clear, even if it's jumbled from Cruce's hurried movements.

I lift my head to look down the hallway toward the master bedroom, horrified to see Cruce stumbling out of it. He lurches all the way across the hall, careens into the wall, and stumbles back the other way. He has his gun in one hand, the other holding the side of his head, and I can't tell if he's injured or not.

My hearing starts to clear just in time to experience Cruce's roar of agonizing fury as he starts to run after us.

Us?

Who the hell has me?

I start to struggle against whoever's shoulder I'm tossed over, but the person is big and strong, and I'm not even fazing him. He's also leaving Cruce behind, and my last glimpse is of him stumbling after us as the man sprints out the front door and moves quickly down the path to the beach.

I dig my hands against my captor's back and push up to look over my shoulder. Several black-dressed men run in front of him.

Two others appear from the darkness on the path behind us. They are dressed in black, too, from head to toe and carry handguns.

I scream for Cruce, but I know it's fruitless. He's one man against several, and he was clearly injured in that blast… whatever it was.

It takes only moments before we emerge onto the beach. The men head straight for the dock and as I twist once again to see what we're running toward, I'm stunned to spot a black inflatable boat with an engine. One of those military-types soldiers train in.

"Get her in the boat," someone yells, and the man carrying me dumps me unceremoniously inside. It's a jarring fall, and my lower back hits something hard.

I ignore it, immediately scrambling toward the edge with the intent to fling myself into the water.

"Oh, no you don't, princess," someone says. A large

hand is in my hair and yanking me back. When he lets go, it sends me sprawling, my t-shirt flying up to expose my nudity.

I don't even have time to be concerned about it, my only thought escape. Once again, I lunge for the side, only to be jerked back viciously by my hair again.

"Try it again and I'm going to hit you," the man promises.

I rise to my knees, lose my balance as I'm still dizzy from that explosion, and press my hands into the bottom of the boat so I don't face plant.

I growl, "Fuck you."

His laugh is so sinister that my blood goes cold. "Later, princess. Promise."

Three men jump into the boat, taking positions around me.

"Go, go, go," someone yells, and I lift my head to see the last two men sprinting down the dock.

A gunshot pierces the air, and one of them crumbles. The other doesn't even slow, turning on the jets to reach the now-running boat. It starts to drift backward from the dock when another gunshot rings out.

Eyes on the beach, I feel my heart miss a beat when I see Cruce running toward us. His feet hit the dock and he takes aim at the man just as he starts to launch himself off the edge toward the boat.

Cruce squeezes the trigger without pausing in his

chase. The man jerks sideways, his hand going to his shoulder. Twisting, he falls into the water.

The large man beside me raises his own gun, aiming it right at Cruce, who's now in a flat-out sprint to reach the end of the dock as the boat starts to pull away.

"No," I scream, launching myself at the man. I grab hold of his arm, jerking it down.

He merely laughs, nodding at one of his teammates. I watch in horror as the man levels his gun, aims at Cruce, and fires off one shot.

Horrified, I stare as Cruce launches his body off the dock toward us. I can't tell if the bullet hits him or not. I only hear his soft grunt as his hands slap against the side of the boat, holding tight for just a moment.

His gaze locks with mine, and it's filled with fierce determination to save me.

"I'm so sorry," I scream at Cruce above the whine of the boat engine. "This is all my fault."

Whether he hears me or not, I don't know. He hauls himself onto the edge of the boat, getting one shoulder up and over the inflatable as we continue to reverse away from the dock.

The man who shot at him originally takes aim once again, right at Cruce's head.

"No," I screech, now trying to lunge for that man. The gun goes off before I can make it to him, and when I whirl around to the front of the boat, Cruce is gone.

I dash for the edge, intent on trying to leap over once again. I have to save Cruce.

A large, meaty arm wraps around my middle and hauls me back. I strain against his hold, searching the darkened water as we pull away from the lighted dock. Cruce never reappears, and hot tears start leaking from my eyes.

It doesn't seem to register that I've been kidnapped, nor that I'm now heading off to a fate that could be worse than death.

Doesn't really matter, though.

Not if Cruce is dead.

"You're a feisty one," the man holding me says appreciatively. "But that spells problems down the road. You're going to need to take a nap for me."

I have no clue what that means. I desperately search the water, seeing nothing but the wake left by the boat.

And then I feel a small prick in my arm. I try to keep my eyes open, hoping to see Cruce's head break the surface near the dock, but it's receding from my view. Whatever that fucker just shot into me works fast, and my head lolls until it falls back on the man's shoulder.

"Blow it," someone says, and I wonder what that means.

There's an explosion, a wave of hot air caresses over me, and I watch almost dispassionately as the boat we'd had docked blazes into a ball of fire.

I close my eyes and fall under, not really caring if I wake back up.

◆

"LET'S GO," SOMEONE says from the doorway. I spin away from the window where I'd been thinking about Cruce.

And crying.

I can't believe he's dead. Part of me refuses to believe it, but the other part knows what I saw. My heart hurts so bad, and I feel like I'm dying.

I've been in a beautiful bedroom in someone's exceptionally expansive mansion. I'd woken up here a few hours ago, at least by account of the battery clock on the bedside table.

I know I'm in a mansion because I can see out the bedroom window on the second floor, and I'm actually in a wing that juts off the main portion. There's an identical wing on the far side, done in brown brick with cream trim. The grounds—rolling hills and pastures—look far-reaching and extensive, not another house in sight.

I have no clue if I'm even in the United States, but the style of the house does seem to be typical American. In addition, my captors all had American accents so through my logic and deductive reasoning, I believe I'm on home soil.

I recognize the man at my door. He's big, burly, and dressed in camo fatigues with a black t-shirt. My guess is he's former military, by virtue of his bearing and command, but the longer hair and goatee means he's private contract.

He's the man who had threatened to hit me, and he shot Cruce as he was hanging on the edge of the boat. He's scarier in daylight, with a jagged scar running down from the bottom of his right eye to his jawline.

"Where are we going?" I ask, crossing my arms over my stomach in stubborn refusal to be a good prisoner.

"We're going to 'shut the fuck up and obey me or I will hurt you,'" he growls, then points toward the door. "Now let's go."

I believe him. I believe he'll hurt me. By the look in his eyes, it's obvious he'd relish it.

I want to bolt for the door, but I force myself to walk slowly to defy him in some small way without getting myself hurt in the process.

After I make it safely past him, he gives me a rough shove through the door. I stumble, my elbow knocking against the doorframe.

Asshole.

I rub it gingerly as I move down the hallway in my bare feet. I'm still wearing the t-shirt I had on when they abducted me, but someone had thrown a pair of gray sweatpants over the foot of the bed I'd woken up in.

They still had a price tag on them.

Surprisingly, they were my size and fit perfectly. I didn't want to be grateful for it, but I was. I'd felt way too exposed in just a t-shirt with no panties underneath, particularly because that asshole walking behind me had made a veiled threat to fuck me in the boat.

I shudder even thinking about it, but I keep my chin lifted high.

"Down the stairs," he directs, and I'm thankful he doesn't touch me again.

When we reach the first floor, he moves past me. I dutifully follow him to a set of double doors stained dark. He gives a slight knock, waits a moment, then opens the right door.

He doesn't enter but rather motions me through.

I'm terrified, but I quickly move into the room, ready to hopefully learn the identity of whoever is behind this. The brute follows close behind me.

At first glance, I see it's an office or study with dark paneled walls, a wooden tray ceiling, and gleaming parquet floors. Shelves filled with books, sculptures, and antiques line the wall, and a thick Persian carpet sits beneath a heavy, masculine desk.

There's a large, leather executive chair on the other side, facing away from me, and it slowly turns around to reveal a man.

A rather ordinary-looking man, except he's impeccably dressed in a light gray silk suit with a dark purple tie. He's on the shorter side... no taller than five-seven would be my guess since his head wasn't even showing above the top of the chair. He's in his mid-to-late sixties with snowy-white hair cut short and precise. He stares with shrewd blue eyes a moment before pushing up from his chair.

"Welcome, Dr. Alexander," he says in a crisp New England accent as he motions with a hand to one of the chairs across from his desk.

"Welcome?" I sneer, not moving a muscle. "I've been kidnapped at gunpoint. My... my..."

My voice cracks, and my eyes prick with wetness. I cough to clear my throat. "The man protecting me was shot and killed."

"An unfortunate by-product," he replies with a dismissive wave of his hand, and for the first time in my life, I want to kill someone.

Him to be precise.

"Now, Dr. Alexander... please sit and let's talk."

I lift my chin, refusing to move.

"Sit, or I will have Paul put you in one of those chairs," the man says with such iciness in his voice that a shiver runs up my spine.

I don't even bother looking over my shoulder at the oaf I now know to be named Paul. Instead, I walk stiffly toward the chair on the right. I take a seat, perching my ass on the very edge and folding my hands in my lap. My spine is straight and locked tight for any battle of words that might come my way.

The older man stares a moment before giving his attention to Paul. "Thank you, Paul. That is all for now."

I don't look back but eventually, I hear Paul's footsteps recede and the door close. Rather than sit back in his chair, the man walks around to me. He comes to stand before me, leaning against the heavy wood of his desk and casually crossing one leg over the other at the ankle, tucking his hands into his dress pants.

"You're a smart woman," he says in a matter-of-fact tone. "You know why you're here."

I do, so I don't feel like this requires a reply.

"It would go a lot easier on you," he continues in a weirdly pleasant, conversational tone, "if you would just give me the formula."

"Who are you?" I demand. "And why do you want it?"

He doesn't appear offended. "I don't think you really want to know that, Dr. Alexander, because I certainly can't let you go at some point if you can identify me."

I don't buy that. I'm not getting out of here alive if they're able to get that formula out of me. But it's clear he's not going to tell me his name.

Still, I press. "You're American. We had assumed a foreign power wanted the science."

"You assumed wrong," he replies blandly. "Now... I

can promise you will be released unharmed if you will share your knowledge with me. If you don't, it's going to hurt."

"I choose hurt," I reply stubbornly, hoping to God I can withstand whatever they have planned for me while internally begging the Jameson group to figure out where I am.

"As you wish," the man says with a sinister glare.

Then he backhands me across the face. It comes so fast I can barely blink before he makes contact.

It's a vicious blow, and it snaps my head so hard to the left that pain shoots up my neck and explodes across my cheekbone. I see stars in my vision and when they start to clear, the man is staring at the gold signet ring on his right hand, presumably checking for any chunks of my skin left behind.

I lift my hand to touch my face, and it comes back with blood on it.

"Paul," the man calls, and the door opens. "Take her to the basement and work on her."

The words make my blood go cold. Tensing, I try to psych myself up—try to pull out all my strength and courage. The minute I give this information up, I'm done for in this world.

As I think it, though... a part of me isn't all that scared by the prospect because at least I would be reunited with Cruce.

CHAPTER 19

Cruce

WHEN MY HEAD breaks the surface of the water, I tread for a few moments, staring out at the remnants of the fiery mess that was my only means to chase after Barrett. I can faintly hear the engine of the inflatable tactical boat moving in the direction of Virgin Gorda.

I swim toward the shore, which wastes precious moments, but there's the minor matter of fire and boat fuel I need to navigate around in the water. My shoulder hurts like a motherfucker where I'd taken a bullet, but it feels like it went all the way through. It takes me at least ten minutes to make it to the beach, and I spend another few moments trying to catch my breath and stay upright against the dizziness caused by blood loss.

Hissing through my teeth, I gently poke at the entrance wound in the front of my shoulder, just below my shoulder blade. Hesitantly, I do the same on my back, feeling a slightly larger hole there. I'm relieved the bullet is out, but I'm worried I might die from blood loss.

However, that's not an option since Barrett is in the hands of people who are deranged and sophisticated enough to pull off a very quick assault and also had the intelligence means to find us. Gritting my teeth, I jog up the path toward the main house.

Once inside, I walk over to the large rectangular fire pit that sits in the middle of the living area. We hadn't touched it yet as we hadn't spent a lot of time in here. It's not designed for heat but rather ambiance as the flames are gas generated and more of the simmering type—meant to cause a romantic glow more than anything.

Without much thought, I turn the gas valve on and use the push button to ignite it. I then head straight to the guest bathroom where I remove Barrett's laptop and notes from the vault behind the painting over the toilet. Whoever struck us tonight didn't have the time to get this. I'm sure they looked for it on the way in and out as best they could, but since I pursued them after recovering from the flash-bang grenade they'd tossed in the room, I had obviously pissed on those plans.

The laptop is crucial—not just for the research but because I have a feeling the answer to how we were found is on it. The words Barrett's had screamed from the boat still echo in my ears.

I'm so sorry. This is all my fault.

I make a quick detour into the master bedroom to

grab the satellite phone that had been on the bedside table. There's a faintly acrid smell from the flash-bang grenade they'd used to incapacitate us when they'd entered, but the room is otherwise unscathed. I grab a pair of shorts out of a dresser drawer and slip them on, groaning from the pain it causes in my shoulder.

I don't bother with a towel for the wound. To temporarily staunch the flow, I'd need to lean up against something for pressure to the back while I held it to the front with my hand. I just don't have time for that.

Instead, I head to the kitchen and press the speed-dial button for Kynan on the phone. He answers on the second ring.

I don't waste time on formalities. "They have Barrett. It was a blitz attack. I need you to get Bebe on the line and into Barrett's computer, so we can figure out what happened. Barrett did something to compromise our location."

"Are you okay?" Kynan asks.

"I've been shot, and they have Barrett," I snap as I open cabinets in the kitchen in search of one thing in particular. "No, I'm not okay. It would help if you can get a chopper headed this way to pick me up, though."

"Call you back in five minutes with chopper details and Bebe on the line," he replies before he disconnects. I'm glad he didn't want to waste time talking about my wounds or what happened.

"Aha," I mutter with profound joy when I find what I'm looking for.

I grab the heavy cast iron skillet from a shelf, a hand towel off the counter, and head into the living room. Shoving the satellite phone into the waistband of my shorts, I set the skillet face down on the stone ledge of the fire pit, placing the handle directly into the flame.

While that's cooking, I pull Barrett's computer onto my lap, lift the top, and press the power button. I know I'm going to be perturbed over what Bebe will find on here, but that's going to be far outweighed by the sickening anxiety I feel over the fact Barrett is now in extreme danger. I absolutely cannot lose her.

Not because she's a client, but because she and I have something together.

Something real and something that will last far beyond all of this.

So, I need to get her back.

Once at her login screen, I easily fill in her credentials. I made her give them to us before we left Jameson, so we could have access to it in case something happened to her. It was a smart move—one I fucking hate I had the foresight for.

When the satellite phone shrills a ring, I nab it, pressing the button to put it on speakerphone so I can keep my hands free. Setting it on the ledge beside me, I glance at the skillet, deciding to give it a few more moments.

"Got the laptop," I say by way of greeting as I move it to the stone ledge beside the phone. "Booting it up now."

"Got Bebe here," Kynan replies. "And a chopper headed your way."

Bebe doesn't spare any pleasantries. "Connect to the Wi-Fi."

It takes just a few seconds to complete. "Done."

"Okay, give me just a few minutes," she mutters, and I can hear her tapping away on her own keyboard through the speaker.

"What's your physical situation?" Kynan asks.

"Bullet through and through just below my clavicle," I say as I pick up the hand towel and use it to grab the edge of the skillet. "Taking care of that now."

Pulling the handle from the flame, I take a deep breath and decide to address the wound on my back first. It's going to be the hardest to reach, and I'm going to be fucking addled with pain after this first attempt.

"How's that?" Kynan asks, but I don't answer.

Instead, I take another breath, grit my teeth, and raise the skillet over my shoulder. I bring it down, twisting my neck as far as I can to get as good a view as possible, then press the red-hot end to where I approximate the wound to be. Luckily, the handle is probably twice as wide as the bullet hole, which increases my odds of getting it right. However, I can't help but scream as the wound starts to burn and sizzle.

"F-u-u-u-c-k," I bellow at the top of my lungs, forcing myself to hold the cast iron to the wound so it can cauterize it closed.

I manage to pull the skillet back up and over my shoulder, feeling as weak as a baby now—not only from the blood loss, but also from the smell of burning flesh and the realization of what I just did to myself. I manage to drop the skillet onto the ledge, placing the end back in the flame to get it hot again.

"Sounds like that hurt," Kynan mutters sympathetically.

Pressing my hand onto the ledge to hold me upright, I take a few deep breaths to try to calm my heart rate. I can still feel blood leaking from the front wound, already dreading going through that process again.

"It looks like Barrett sent out two emails yesterday," Bebe says brusquely, and that helps to distract me a bit. "One to her research assistant asking him to check something she needed to finalize her theory. She only logged on for an extremely brief time before she logged right back off. I can see on his end that he read it, but he didn't forward it to anyone else. Instead, he replied directly to her about ten minutes later. Barrett logged back on about an hour later, read the answer, then sent a second email to her uncle telling him she'd finished the formula. Her total time online was incredibly short."

"Then how the fuck did they find us?" I ask.

"It would be almost impossible given the minimal amount of time she was online," Bebe muses, still tapping away on a keyboard on her end. "But let me check something… hold on."

I glance back at the skillet. Might as well knock that out.

While Bebe works her magic, I grab the hot iron once again. After taking a few seconds to psych myself up, I cauterize the front wound with the hot metal. I manage to keep my teeth clamped down, but there's no stopping the pained groan I emit as I fight the nausea brought on by the smell of burning flesh.

"Sounds like that one hurt like a mother," Kynan comments as I pant through the pain.

"I'm fine," I grit out, but I'm on the verge of passing out. I toss the skillet onto the floor, then press my palm down again onto the stone ledge so I don't topple over.

"This is interesting," Bebe says, and I blink hard a few times. It helps to reorient me.

"What's that?" I ask as I look down at the wound on my chest and it's blackened with red blisters around the edge. At least it's not bleeding.

"I checked the server at her lab," she replies succinctly. "It wasn't compromised in any way."

"But the one to her uncle?" Kynan prompts.

"Again, I can't find any indication it's compromised," she says. "And I imagine hacking the president's email is impossible, although it would be a challenge I would certainly find interesting."

"Bebe," I snap, a little cranky right now... given everything going on. Barrett being kidnapped, me being shot, and everything else.

"Sorry," she mutters under her breath. "At any rate, there is something very suspicious."

"What's that?" I ask.

"Well, shortly after the president received the email, a phone call went out of the West Wing. By reverse scanning the staff directory, it looks like it was one of his senior aides, Deputy Chief of Staff of Operations, Winston Carnes."

"So?" I push. That could easily be coincidental.

"Then, not long after the call ended, some type of code was deployed on the servers that sent out a ping."

"A ping?"

"A beacon... one that can reverse crawl the same pathway the email to the president had taken."

"Back to the source," Kynan mutters.

"Right to Marjorie Island," I add, shaking my head in bewilderment. It doesn't make sense. "I don't believe President Alexander is involved in this. He'd never do anything to harm Barrett."

"You might be right," Kynan says, obviously choosing his words carefully. "But we can't discount it."

"No," I say adamantly. "It's not him. It's Winston Carnes. That's who's responsible."

A choppy vibration rumbles overhead. With a long-suffering sigh, I rise to a standing position. "The chopper's here," I say.

"We've got a private jet on the runway in Virgin Gorda to bring you here," Kynan replies.

"Not to Pittsburgh," I say. "Straight to D.C. You can meet me there."

Kynan curses under his breath before saying, "I'm not sure you're in the best position—"

"Just fucking meet me in D.C.," I snap. "And bring me some clothes."

"You were shot, for fuck's sake," Kynan growls. "You've been under extreme duress. I can handle—"

"Not up for debate," I bark over him. "Meet me in D.C."

I don't give him a chance to reply before I disconnect the satellite phone. Picking up Barrett's laptop and notepad, I head out the front door and maneuver down the path to the beach where the chopper will land to pick me up. I don't bother with our belongings or any of my equipment. Kynan can send someone back for that.

I don't believe President Alexander is involved in this in any way. I know the man as well as most people close to him do, even better yet since spending time with Barrett over the last few days. I've heard enough about how he stepped in after her parents died to be a surrogate father and mentor to her. The man loves her unconditionally, and she feels the same.

He's not involved.

But Winston Carnes must know something. And because time is of the essence—because every precious minute that ticks by means Barrett could be a minute closer to death—I'm going to make sure I get the truth from him as quickly as I can.

CHAPTER 20

Cruce

I F THERE IS any other proof I'd need that President Alexander isn't connected in any way to the kidnapping of his niece, him cancelling his afternoon meetings—including one with the Chairman of the Joint Chiefs of Staff about current operations going on in northern Syria that have been dominating the news lately—assures me of his innocence.

"You need to keep your cool," Kynan advises me as we follow an aide down a corridor in the West Wing.

"I'm fine," I mutter as I roll my left shoulder, which feels like it has been pounded with a wrecking ball.

Kynan met me at Dulles where my charter flight landed after a quick refuel in Miami. He not only had a change of clothes for me, but he also had Dr. Corinne Ellery—our resident psychiatrist—in tow.

While I was anxious to get changed and head to the White House, Kynan insisted I let her treat my wounds.

I grumbled about it the entire time, as did Dr. Ellery.

"This was not part of the job I was hired to do for

Jameson," she had complained. "I'm a psychiatrist. I treat the mind, not the body."

"But you went to medical school," Kynan had replied, "and until such time as I can hire someone else, you're just going to have to step up. And besides... I don't get what the problem is."

She had grimaced as she checked my wounds, applying some betadine and clean gauze to them front and back. "Because you'll start me off with cauterized gunshot wounds. Then, next thing I know, it'll snowball and you'll want me to perform an emergency amputation or something."

"I just need you to give him some antibiotics, so it doesn't get infected," Kynan muttered in response. "And make sure he won't bleed to death until we can get Barrett back."

Which is exactly what she did, administering a shot of Levaquin with a Prednisone booster in the top part of my ass cheek. She also handed me a bottle of oral antibiotics to take. I'd shoved them in the pocket of my cargo pants and promised I would take them, but, frankly, it wasn't my main priority.

The aide reaches the Oval Office and gives a sharp rap on the door, entering without waiting for an answer. It's clear we're expected and with all haste.

President Alexander rises from his chair behind his desk as Kynan and I walk in. He moves around it, approaching me with an angst-filled expression. Holding his hand out to me, he asks, "How are you doing? Kynan said you were shot."

I shake his hand, trying not to wince as his free hand comes to my left shoulder for a light clap. I ignore his question about my state of health. "I'm sorry I let you down, sir."

The president doesn't seem to like me saying that. He squeezes my shoulder once more, and I can't help but flinch before pulling away. Immediately understanding it's my wounded side, he utters a curse I know is actually quite uncharacteristic of the man.

"Christ... I'm sorry, Cruce," he says as he motions us toward the couches. "I'm just so worried about Barrett."

He then pins me with a harsh glare. "And don't you dare apologize again. Kynan filled me in on what happened, and there was nothing you could have done to prevent it. The fact you put yourself in such danger to try to save her has me once again in your debt."

I wave him off. Instead, I move to the heart of why I wanted to come to D.C. in the first place. I don't bother with taking a seat as was politely suggested. Pacing, I ask, "What can you tell us about Winston Carnes?"

Kynan and I had decided not to fill the president in on what we knew over the phone as we wanted to be there in person to see his reaction. The only thing he knows is Barrett was located and taken by some unknown force after she sent the email to him.

"Winston? Why do you want to know about Winston?" he asks, brows furrowed.

"Just answer the question, sir," I reply tersely.

The president's eyebrows shoot upward. I expect had this been any other situation, I'd receive a severe dressing down for my temerity. But he gets the urgency. "Winston's been with me since I took office. He's one of my senior aides... currently Deputy Chief of Staff for Operations."

"You didn't bring him over from when you were VP," I point out, meaning I don't know the man at all.

Alexander shakes his head. "No. Actually, he was recommended to me by Chief of Staff Lydia Forrester."

"And does he have access to your email?" Kynan asks.

The president swings his head Kynan's way. "Not my official government email. But he does my personal email. He's sort of like a social secretary in a way. He checks my personal email for me as I don't have time some days. Forwards me the important stuff and has the authority to respond to some things without me."

"And he read the email from Barrett?" I hazard a guess.

Alexander nods. "Yes. In fact, he brought it right to my attention. Printed me off a copy."

Kynan and I exchange a look, prompting the president to ask, "Do you think he's responsible for Barrett's kidnapping?"

"We don't know," I say truthfully, but it sure looks that way. "After the email was read, he called out on his extension to a number registered to a flower shop."

"And what could that possibly mean?" the president asks, frowning with confusion.

"Might mean nothing, except that a few moments later, some type of spyware was deployed from the servers here in the Oval Office to trace backward to the source of the email. It's how Barrett and I were located."

"Son of a bitch," President Alexander mutters as he drags his hand through his hair. He glances between me and Kynan before settling on me. "Should I get Lydia Forrester in here? He worked for her in the private sector before I brought her on as chief of staff."

"No," Kynan replies with a shake of his head. "Given their ties before coming to work for you, they could be in collusion."

"I just can't believe this," Alexander says in a voice that sounds as lost as he looks. He walks to the couch, sits down heavily, and sighs. "People in my own office?"

"We want to talk to Winston Carnes," I say. "Can you call him in here?"

"Of course," the president replies. He pops right back off the couch, eager to do something that will progress this all forward.

Kynan and I stand by silently as Alexander hurries to

his desk phone and pushes a button that rings through to Carnes' extension. It comes through on the speaker.

"Yes, sir," Carnes answers crisply.

"Can you come into my office?" Alexander asks, his voice a mask of calm perfection despite the fact he must be bristling on the inside.

"Of course, sir. Be right there."

Alexander disconnects. In no more than thirty seconds, there's a knock on the door before it opens.

Winston Carnes is thirty-four years old, but he looks about twenty. Kynan and I had his basic resume, including info on where he was born, education, and family ties through a social media search, all thanks to Bebe's quick skills. He shares the same political leanings as his president, as expected, so it's a little hard to accept Barrett has been in danger from someone this close to the Oval Office.

Still... I shot a Secret Service agent who was supposed to protect Alexander, so traitors do indeed exist.

Regardless, Carnes is single, lives with four cats, and doesn't appear to have much of a social life. He's skinny, pale, and doesn't appear overly confident, but he'll use his brain to try to outsmart us. My guess is if he's working against Barrett, it's at someone's behest. If so, I'd rather know that information sooner rather than later.

Carnes' eyes go to the president first, then to me, and

finally to Kynan, where he gives us a polite nod. He holds an iPad with a digital pen poised. "Yes, sir. What can I do for you?"

I don't have time for polite conversation, nor do I think it would be effective. Instead, I choose brute force.

Stalking up to Carnes, I slap the iPad out of his hand. The tablet crashes to the floor. While it doesn't break into a million pieces because Apple makes structurally sound products, I'm quite sure it's broken.

There's a moment of stunned silence where I take the opportunity to grab Carnes by the lapels of his suit and swing him around. Shoving him backward toward the wall, I slam his body into it. His head snaps backward, and the painting on the wall shudders. He grunts from the force of the impact against his kidneys.

In surprised annoyance, Kynan barks, "For fuck's sake," while lunging at me.

President Alexander shouts, "Cruce!"

And two different doors leading into the Oval Office fly open, Secret Service agents pouring in with weapons drawn.

I don't move a muscle, merely hold Carnes in place with my face right in his, glaring harshly.

"It's okay," the president exclaims, presumably to the agents. "It's fine. I want everyone out of here right now."

I can hear footsteps receding and doors closing. Kynan stands at my back, not saying a word. The fact

Alexander just chased everyone out of his office implied I had permission to move forward with intimidation tactics.

At least that's the way I'm taking it.

"Now," I murmur, as if I'm having a nice, private conversation with Carnes. "Tell me who you work for and why you want Barrett Alexander."

"I-I-I-don't know what you mean," he stutters in response, but all I hear is lies.

I'm all for efficiency. I need him to clearly understand I'm not going to take my time working up to the point where I'm tired of asking questions.

I haul my right hand back, then cock it at my hip. With a hard twist of my hips, I deliver a vicious upper cut to his stomach. I catch him just below the breastbone, driving upward.

Carnes doubles over, gasping for breath and moaning. I grab him by the hair, forcing his head back. He looks at me with tears leaking out of his eyes. "I am not going to stop hitting you. Not until you break and tell me what I need to know. I'm going to get the truth from you, and no one in this office is going to stop me or save you. And once my knuckles get sore, I'm going to start cutting you. And if you make me work hard for it, the president is going to make sure you get absolutely no leniency from the federal prosecutors. It means you're facing decades, if not life, behind bars for whatever your involvement is. But if you make this easy on us, because we're all very worried about Barrett, then we will let the prosecutors know you cooperated. If your cooperation helps us get Barrett back unharmed, I'm sure the president will be incredibly grateful."

Carnes wheezes, his eyes wide and bulging as they cut over to Alexander and then back to me.

"Now," I say very calmly. "Those are your choices. What's it going to be?"

"It's Clarence Scavino," he blurts out.

I jerk in surprise, honestly figuring it would have taken a few more punches to get him softened enough to spill his guts. Maybe something is finally fucking going right.

I glance over my shoulder at the president. He appears perplexed. "He's the deputy director of the National Economic Council."

I whip around to Carnes, giving him a tiny shake by the lapels. "What's his interest in Barrett?"

Carnes doesn't hesitate in his reply now that he's given up who he takes orders from. "Everyone knows it's the president's agenda to share free energy breakthroughs with other countries."

"So?" Kynan replies, stepping up beside me. Carnes' attention shifts to him.

"So," Carnes drawls, tone implying we're stupid. "It's not in our country's best interests to alleviate the dependency of other countries upon us. Making others stronger weakens our power."

"That's ridiculous," the president sputters.

"Is it?" Carnes asks, focusing on Alexander. "We are the most powerful country in the world because we own everything, including the allegiance of others since they depend on us."

"I don't buy it." Alexander sneers, marching up to Carnes. He studies the traitor, who is still held in my clutches, then shakes his head at Kynan. "Scavino doesn't have the money to pull something like this off."

"Then he's not the head of the snake," I surmise, studying Carnes. "Who is it? Who do you and Scavino answer to?"

"I don't know," Carnes replies quickly, holding his arms up. "I swear. I just know he has big money backing him."

"To commit treason," President Alexander growls. To my utter surprise, he throws a punch at Carnes, hitting him square in the bridge of his nose.

Blood spurts out, splattering my chest, and Carnes squeals like a pig. Once again, the doors burst open as agents rush in.

This time, Alexander doesn't wave them off. Instead, he nods toward Carnes. "Take him into custody, then call the FBI to place him under arrest for treason. And I'm sure a host of other charges, too."

The agents move in as Carnes screams. "You promised if I helped, I'd get recognition of that."

"And you will," the president replies as they start to pull Carnes away. "As long as what you've provided leads to us finding Barrett quickly and safely."

"Malcolm," Alexander says to one of the agents who steps forward. He and I shared protective detail when Alexander was vice president and he chose to stay on. He's a good man. "I want you to go to Clarence Scavino's office. Take him into custody. We'll turn him over to the FBI but for right now, I want him isolated from all people and access to phones or computers."

"Yes, sir," he replies without asking for any other details. He sharply pivots, then heads out of the office.

When we're alone, Alexander turns to Kynan and me. "Not much we can do right now except wait for federal prosecutors and the FBI to step in and interview Scavino."

"You should have let us take a crack at him," I gripe.

Alexander shakes his head. "This is high treason, Cruce. It goes beyond just Barrett now. It's about contravening presidential policy as well as the law. I have to go by the books."

"When will they talk to him?" I ask.

His expression is grim. "Soon. Probably within the hour. But he'll lawyer up."

"Fuck," I grunt, wanting to ram my fist through the

wall.

"Bebe," Kynan says, but him saying her name doesn't make sense to me.

"Huh?"

"Bebe," he says again. "Let's get Bebe to start digging digitally. Let her hack Scavino's computer, phone records, and bank accounts. It might take her a few hours, but it's better than nothing."

"No, wait," I say with a sudden burst of inspiration. "Call back your men on Scavino. Let's set him up to force him to call his money benefactor."

"How's that?" Alexander asks, but Kynan nods his agreement without me needing to explain.

"We spook him," I reply. "Get Carnes to tell him that we were nosing around asking questions about Barrett's kidnapping. He can tell Scavino he's scared, but then assure him that he kept his mouth shut. That could make him reach out to warn whoever is actually running this show."

Alexander doesn't hesitate. He exits the Oval Office, and I get an image of him sprinting down the hall to catch up with the agents he'd just dispatched to grab Scavino.

To Kynan, I say, "You need to assemble a strike team ASAP. We could be ready to move on this guy to find Barrett very soon."

He pulls his phone out to make the call. "I already

had them come to D.C. They're on standby. I'll get them here."

I move over to look out the set of three tall windows behind the president's desk, staring blankly at the Rose Garden that borders the exterior of the Oval Office. There's a chance I'd see Barrett shortly.

Hold her in my arms.

This should alleviate my worry, but it doesn't. They've had her for over twelve hours, which is a hell of a long time to implement torture techniques to make someone talk. I can only hope and pray the grit and determination she has within her is enough to fortify her resolve to hold onto her secrets.

Because once she tells them what they want to know, they will have no further use for her.

CHAPTER 21

Barrett

M Y TEETH CHATTER ceaselessly.

So damn cold down here.

It's a regular basement as best I can tell, but the room they put me in must be soundproofed because it's deadly quiet when the door is closed. I can't hear any noises whatsoever.

They've also left me in absolute darkness. Not even a thin line of light under the door from the outside can be seen.

It's almost like a sensory-deprivation chamber given I can't see or hear anything, but I sure as hell can feel the cold, so not quite.

No clue how long I've been in here. Feels like hours, but I'm so uncomfortable it wouldn't surprise me if it's only been minutes. That oaf Paul put me in a folding metal chair, then tied my hands behind my back and my ankles to the metal legs. I tested the strength of the rope bonds, but there was no wiggle room. When he left, the resounding sound of metal sliding against metal told me there was more than just a standard lock on the door. I would not be leaving from this side on my own, so I stopped struggling with the ropes to conserve my energy.

But then the cold seeped in, my arms and legs alternating between cramping pain and absolute numbness. My mind starts playing tricks on me because it's so silent in the inky black darkness.

The worst part of being down here in the freezing solitude is it gives me plenty of time to think about Cruce. About him taking that crazy jump from the dock onto the side of the boat—knowing they had guns and he'd be shot. But it never even slowed him down. He didn't hesitate to expend all his zeal to save me, despite the fact it would cost him his own life.

So I think about how brave he was and how I'll never know what we could have had together. It makes me cry, and I can't seem to stop. My tears feel frozen on my cold cheeks, but of all my discomforts, nothing compares to the searing pain in the center of my chest from losing Cruce.

He was my chance at happiness.

I had always thought I was a happy person before meeting him because I loved my work and career. Cruce made me realize how much I've been missing in life, but it disappeared in a heartbeat when his stopped beating.

The screech of metal sliding against metal—so ominous sounding that my heart thuds like a giant drum—

pierces the silence, and I jerk against my bonds. My sadness over Cruce vanishes as fear takes root deep in my gut.

I strain to see toward the area I believe the door to be in, then a flood of light blinds me as it opens. My eyes involuntarily snap shut against the pain of it, yet my fear won't let me sit here in continued darkness. I wince, opening my eyes up a fraction to see who's coming through that door.

I see nothing but a large outline of a man with wide shoulders and powerful legs. I'm assuming it's Paul, although it could be anyone. Whoever has kidnapped me has the money and means to hire a small mercenary army to do his bidding as evidenced by how quickly and effectively they struck. It could be any one of those murderers, which is what they all are. Maybe only one pulled the trigger and shot Cruce, but they're all responsible for his death.

A light comes on overhead. As I start to become accustomed to it, my vision focuses. It's Paul, and I don't like the look in his eyes.

Way too much determination.

He's here for the information I hold in my head.

Cruce had warned me about this if I were to be captured. Our second night on the island, over dinner, he had a terrifying conversation with me about what would happen if I were caught.

Paramount, he'd said, would be to get the information from me at all costs. He'd informed me in a cold, flat tone that they would hurt me to get it.

He also told me to resist the impulse to give in because once they had the information, chances were they would kill me. They were never going to let a witness who could identify them live to do so.

I try to straighten my spine to show my defiance, but Paul just smirks. Apparently, I amuse him.

"They say you are a brilliant scientist," he murmurs as he approaches. My eyes stay locked on his. When he reaches my chair, he squats so we are eye to eye. "So you are surely smart enough to know what I want."

"I won't give you anything," I say. It takes everything within me to keep my voice calm and confident.

Paul's glare bores deep into mine, perhaps trying to glean just how much I mean that.

He merely inclines his head. "We shall see."

And so, it begins.

Paul stands, then moves over to a metal table against one wall. He pulls it toward me, the legs scraping along the concrete floor. The sound is excruciating to my ears after having been left in silence so long.

When he drops it beside me, I twist to see, fearing the horrible instruments of torture that might rest there. Instead, I'm surprised to find the top bare.

Paul pulls his phone out of his pocket, taps the

screen a few times, then sets it beside me on the table. He explains, "I'm recording our little session. Can't cause you pain and take notes on what you're going to tell me at the same time, you know."

I flash a faux smile. "Let the record reflect I think you're an asshole, and you probably have a little dick, too."

Paul may be big and appear to be an oaf, but he's surprisingly quick. I don't even see his hand coming at me, but I sure feel the crack of his palm against my cheek. My head snaps to the right, and my face explodes with pain. It's the second time in mere hours I've been hit. The other strike was a backhand from a righty, so it was to my right cheek. This one was also from a righty, but he wound up like he was taking a swing for the fences and hit me with an open palm on my left cheek. I had thought nothing could hurt worse than knuckles, but I was wrong. Paul's youth and size over the older man makes a world of difference in the pain scale.

My eyes immediately water, and I'm sufficiently cowed for a moment. In fact, I keep my face averted and stare at the floor, too afraid to look at him.

I've never been struck in my life. My parents were averse to any physical forms of punishment. I've never had a man lay a hand on me or been in a fight with another woman. In fact, I've led a relatively uninjured and healthy life unless you count the time in fourth grade when I broke my ring finger on my right hand after falling off the monkey bars. I think it was then I realized I was better suited to academia rather than outdoor activities.

"Let's try this again," Paul says pleasantly, his hand comes to the top of my head. His fingers flex, dig in, and grab a hunk of my hair. He forces my head around to make me look at him. Bending at the waist, he puts his face near mine and murmurs, "Tell me about the formula you finished. I'll need all the details, of course."

"I'm not going to tell you anything," I tell him and then cringe in anticipation of another blow, squeezing my eyes shut tightly.

But it doesn't come.

Hesitantly, I open my eyes to find that Paul had straightened his body. He shakes his head, smiling almost devilishly. "Not going to hit you again, Dr. Alexander. It hurts me as much as it hurts you, and I mean that literally. Oh, no... I've got something a little easier on me and a lot harder on you if you don't start talking."

Oh, God. Him hitting me was bad enough, but knowing he has something worse planned he's apparently going to relish ratchets up my terror level. Still, I keep my mouth clamped shut.

"Suit yourself," Paul says, then squats once again. He starts untying my legs from the chair and for a moment,

I consider kicking him in the face and running. I even go as far as rolling my ankles once they're loose, but the immediate onset of pins and needles has me changing course. Gritting my teeth, I wait through the pain as Paul moves to the back of the chair to remove the bindings from my wrists.

I'm not given a chance to work out any kinks or stiff muscles. Immediately, Paul's hand is back in my hair and he's physically pulling me out of the chair by it. In his other hand, he holds the rope that was around my wrists. I can't help but cry out in pain, and it's all too clear Paul has no qualms about hurting a woman.

In fact, I'd say he's very much enjoying this.

My legs are numb and weak, but Paul refuses to let me sag. If I want to prevent my hair from being torn out of my head, I have to stay upright and follow along behind him.

In the middle of the room, I notice a thick chain with a rusted hook on the end as big as a salad plate hanging from the ceiling. I have no clue what he has planned for me, but I know whatever it is, I need to be moving away from that chain and hook. Pulling away, I ignore the pain in my scalp. Digging my bare feet down into the concrete, I try to jerk myself loose.

"Oh no you don't," Paul says nonchalantly, merely tightening his grip and exerting a bit more force. I'm not strong enough to break free. In no time, I'm standing right under the chain.

He lets go of my hair while ordering, "Hands together."

I glare, unwilling to help him torture me.

"Look down at my hip," Paul says conversationally, a light smile on his face.

I lower my eyes and see what he wants me to see. A knife in a hip holster.

"Now, put your hands together or I'm going to put a few carvings into your face."

The threat is said so softly, and without any real malice, that it makes it even more terrifying and believable. I slam my hands together so hard they make a resounding clap.

Paul grins as he wraps the rope tightly around my wrists, finishing with a triple knot.

"Up you go," he says. Before I can comprehend what that means, he's jerking my arms up, pulling me right up to my tiptoes, and slipping my bound wrists over the edge of the hook. I try to go flat-footed, but the ropes are too tight and there's no give in them. As such, I'm stuck not quite on the very tips of my toes, but most of my weight is on the balls of my feet. If I try to lower myself, it pulls horribly on my shoulders.

Once I'm secure, Paul doesn't say another word. He merely pivots away from me and leaves the room. From the balls of my feet, I manage to swing myself around to look at the door. He'd left it open, and I immediately try to get my wrists over the hook so I can free myself. I can't quite extend far enough, though, and I growl in frustration.

"That's cute." Paul laughs as he walks back through the door with something in his hand.

It looks like a white pole about two feet long with a gripped handle and a rectangular box about a quarter of the way down. He'd said hitting me with his hands was too hard on him, so he clearly got something to assist. Tears prick my eyes as I wonder just how strong I can be once he starts.

"Now," Paul drawls as he stands before me, holding the pole loosely in one hand. "I'm going to ask you nicely to tell me all your secrets just one more time."

I don't reply, forcing myself to look him in the eye as a means of clear but silent defiance.

Sighing, Paul gives a careless shrug. "Oh, well."

He raises the pole, and I can't help but brace against what I'm assuming is going to be a bone-jarring blow somewhere on my body. To my surprise, though, he merely places the end of it against my thigh.

I have only a moment of confusion, wondering what in the hell he's doing, when a sizzling pain shoots up and down my leg, then into my lower back and stomach. Shrieking from surprise and because it's the worst thing I've ever felt in my life, I try to jerk my body away from it.

It lasts only a second or two before Paul pulls the rod

away. He grins, holding it up before his face, and I can now see the end is forked with metal probes on the bottom.

"Genius little contraption," he murmurs, almost proudly. "It's a cattle prod, but this one has been upgraded a bit. In fact, you're getting almost four times the usual juice by virtue of this little booster here."

He taps the rectangular box and I'll admit, the energy scientist part of me is curious. I'd like to know just how many volts I just took because that hurt more than I can even describe.

"Now," he says ominously. "I only touched you with that for a few seconds, but I'm going to hold it to you a lot longer each time you don't talk. If we're not careful, your flesh is going to start cooking. So why don't you just do yourself a favor and tell me what I want to know."

He's fucking sadistic to the core, clearly enjoying this new form of torture. He could probably break a few bones of mine to make me start spilling everything, but he wants this to go on for no other reason than he enjoys it.

Paul stares, one eyebrow rising just a tad. "Are you scared? Want to talk?"

I give a tiny shake of my head, knowing I'm getting ready to be tested like very few are ever tested in their lifetime. I hope to God I'm strong enough to take it.

CHAPTER 22

Cruce

"**Y**OU HAD BETTER not fuck this up," I warn Carnes as he sits in a chair with his hands cuffed in front of him. Although he's as far away from a flight risk as I can imagine, the FBI are not taking any chances and are running things by the book.

For the past hour, Kynan has been working with Carnes on what to say to Scavino. It's taken this long because Carnes is a nervous wreck.

It's why Kynan shoots me an exasperated look for threatening the man when he's trying to get him to calm down.

"We're ready to wire him," one of the FBI agents says.

We're in a private conference room in the West Wing that's been commandeered as a base of operations. The president has gone back to the Oval Office to attend to his duties, but we're under strict orders to notify him before Carnes goes into Scavino's office so he can be present to listen in on the wire.

Probably the best thing he did before he left was sit down and talk with Carnes. He spoke to him like a father to a son, like he was disappointed in some stupid stunt Carnes had pulled. He even put his hand on his shoulder, imploringly telling Carnes the best way he could fix everything was to do whatever it took to help save Barrett's life. I could tell Alexander wasn't sincere in this exaggerated, fatherly type concern just as I could tell Carnes really had no clue Barrett's life was in danger. He'd admitted he knew she'd be kidnapped, but Scavino had assured him it was only to get her formula and she'd be released safely afterward.

The guy is a fucking moron for believing that, but I do trust he's been honest with us so far. Which is good because it's probably our best chance to locate Barrett as quickly as possible.

Within this room, there are several FBI agents, a federal prosecutor, and some of the Jameson crew who has assembled for a rescue operation. Cage and Saint are here from the Pittsburgh office. Kynan ordered Benji Darden and Tank Richardson to put a crew together to stay on standby in Vegas in case Barrett wasn't on the East Coast. The FBI has a unit standing by in Los Angeles as well.

Regardless, we have a sanctioned FBI crew going in with us as backup here from D.C., and I'm praying to God she's close by. Everyone is gearing up while Bebe multitasks on two computers. She's working on hacking Scavino's records while also setting up the back end of the wiretap for the Scavino Sting.

That's what we're calling it anyway.

I'd have preferred to send Carnes in there an hour ago when I came up with this idea, but not only did Carnes need prepped, Bebe also had to get everything set up exactly right. She has to not only monitor what Scavino does, but she also needs to intercept any outgoing calls he might make. She's in a delicate position of needing to identify the person Scavino will call if Carnes can spook him appropriately, pinging the physical location, then stopping the call from actually connecting. If Scavino alerts the person he calls that their operation is in jeopardy, they're going to have plenty of time to kill Barrett and dispose of her body.

This will all boil down to just how good Bebe's skills are, then it will be up to Jameson to move in for the rescue. I only hope to fuck Barrett's somewhere close by because while she's alive only as long as she keeps a hold of her secrets, every minute that ticks by puts her more at risk of giving in. The thought of her being exposed to all means of vile torture techniques has kept my stomach locked in a painful clench and my chest aching with sadness.

I can't lose her.

"Deep thoughts you got going on there, brother?"

Saint asks as he comes up to my side, clapping a hand on my shoulder. I give a last glance at Carnes as an FBI agent removes the cuffs so they can start to wire him up to listen in on his conversation with Scavino.

I shrug with a nonchalance I don't feel at all. "Just worried about the timing of all this. Bebe can't let that call connect. And I hope to fuck Barrett's close by so we can move fast to rescue her."

"We?" he asks with his eyebrows rising.

"Yeah… *we*," I reply emphatically.

"You were just shot," he says with quiet concern. "I think it's best—"

"—for you to keep your fucking mouth shut," I growl. "I'm going, and that's that."

Saint knows when to back down from an unwinnable fight. Smiling, he raises his hands up in surrender. "Understood. But you're taking this very personally."

"Barrett was under *my* watch," I say. "Of course it's personal."

"Shouldn't be *that* personal," he points out.

"What do you mean?"

Saint moves in a bit closer, lowering his voice. "I'm just saying… you look more than a little worried. In fact, you don't look good at all. I'm thinking that's got little to do with your gunshot wounds and everything to do with a brainy, sexy scientist."

I blink in surprise. How can he tell there's something

deeper in my underlying concern? I felt like I'd been keeping things pretty close to the vest.

"I don't know what you're talking about," I mutter. And wait a minute... had he just called Barrett "sexy"? What the fuck?

I glare, but he's not buying it. In fact, he smiles in a way that tells me he understands more than I'd ever give him credit for.

"You fell for her, didn't you?" he murmurs.

I want to scream in denial, but I can't. Why would I ever deny someone as amazing and wonderful as Barrett?

"Yeah... I fell for her," I admit, rubbing hard at the back of my neck. Then I glance over at Kynan where he watches Carnes as he's wired up. "Think he knows?"

Saint grins. "Oh yeah... it's pretty obvious."

"I'll hand in my resignation after we rescue Barrett," I mutter, knowing there will be consequences.

Pulling his chin inward, Saint asks, "Whatever the fuck for? You didn't do anything wrong."

I frown. "I fraternized with a client."

Saint snorts. "First... if what you were doing was 'fraternizing,' then dude... you got to work on your moves. Second... did it compromise Barrett's safety?"

"No," I admit. "If anything, I gave it more effort, and it pisses me off it still wasn't good enough. I let her get taken on my watch, and I'm not sure if I even deserve her."

"Well, that's something between the two of you. I suggest we rescue her first, then you can worry about that."

"Agreed," I reply stiffly, putting my head back in game mode.

"We're ready," Kynan says as Carnes stands from his chair. He looks like he's about to throw up. Kynan turns to one of the Secret Service agents. "Can you get the president?"

The agent nods in acknowledgment, pivots on his heel, and leaves.

Kynan moves to stand in front of Carnes, dipping his head to get closer to him. "You good on how to play this?"

Carnes swallows hard and nods.

"Good. You do this right and help us recover Barrett safely, and that will go a long way to help you out of this shirt storm you've landed yourself in."

Carnes nods again.

Frankly, I don't give a flying fuck what happens to him after this. I've got bigger fish to fry.

"Let's do it, then," Kynan says, giving Carnes a tiny shove toward the door.

◆

CARNES IS IN Scavino's office, waiting patiently for him to finish a phone call. We stationed four FBI agents outside the office, prepared to swoop in and arrest him as soon as the call connects. It could happen within seconds of Carnes leaving or it might never happen. It's a risk we're taking with this path, but Bebe's also working hard on Scavino's accounts, so hopefully something will pan out there if this doesn't work.

The rest of the agents and the Jameson crew are still in the conference room, gathered around some hi-def speakers to listen in. Bebe is poised over her laptop, fingers ready to do whatever magic she needs to identify and intercept the call we hope Scavino will make.

We all go on high alert when Scavino's voice comes across the speaker, wrapping up his phone call. We can't see what's going on, but based on Scavino's tone of impatience, I can imagine he's frowning across his desk at Carnes.

"What can I do for you, Mr. Carnes?" Scavino asks briskly, making it clear he doesn't really have the time.

"I think they're on to us," Carnes says, and his voice is high pitched and squeaky. He sounds incredibly nervous, but that actually works in this case.

"On to us?" Scavino replies vaguely.

As instructed, Carnes doesn't withhold details, making it clear exactly what's at stake since we're recording this. "I just had a meeting with some attorneys at DOJ. They're investigating what they term as 'suspicious' activity on the West Wing servers, and they wanted to examine my computer."

"Did you let them?" Scavino asks, his tone now harsh but concerned. No one wants the Department of Justice sniffing around illegal, treasonous activity.

"They had a warrant," Carnes whines in response.

"Shit," Scavino growls, and I can only imagine the panic in his expression. He knows if they have Carnes' computer, they will find the tracking code that would search out the president's niece where she was hidden in the Caribbean.

It could go one of two ways at this point. Scavino could be suspicious and grill Carnes about this more. If he were smart, he would demand more details as to the types of questions DOJ supposedly asked. If he did, he'd probably sniff out this was a sting operation pretty soon because Carnes isn't particularly good at this stuff.

Or Scavino can panic and react, which seems to be the route he chooses.

"Get out of my office," Scavino orders Carnes.

"Who are you calling, sir?" Carnes asks, and I have to give the fuckwad credit... that's an important alert to us that we didn't ask him to do. Without eyes inside the room, we have to rely solely on Bebe to track and hack the phone call from Scavino. Not only is she going to identify the person to whom the call is going, but she's also going to block the incoming number so the recipient doesn't know who's calling. It might mean the person on the end won't answer if an identifiable number or contact isn't shown on screen, but it's a chance we're going to have to take. We can't give this person any indication anything is wrong.

Carnes just gave us a heads-up Scavino has a phone in hand, ready to make a call.

Bebe moves quickly, tapping on her keyboard.

"I'm calling none of your damn business," Scavino barks, and I can imagine him pointing at his door. "Now... get out. And I suggest you keep your fucking mouth shut. I'll handle all of this."

"Yes, sir," Carnes says, the relief in his voice a little too dramatized. I hope it doesn't make him suspicious.

There's a shuffling sound, presumably Carnes leaving, then Bebe murmurs, "There's an outgoing call."

Her fingers start tapping furiously, lines of code scrolling across her machine.

The ringing of a phone comes across the speakers... once, twice, three times before it connects.

"Hello," we hear. The only thing easily identified is the voice is male.

"Gotcha, you bastard," Bebe exclaims victoriously as she punches a few keys.

Then Scavino's voice, "Richard... DOJ is on to us."

There's silence because Bebe effectively disconnected the call.

"Hello," Scavino says. "Richard... are you there?"

"Move," Kynan orders softly into a headset he's wearing that puts him in direct contact with FBI agents outside Scavino's office.

We can hear the door to Scavino's office flying open, then him crying out in surprise. "What the hell is this?"

"Clarence Scavino… turn around and place your hands behind your back. You're under arrest for treason, kidnapping, and conspiracy."

Bebe reaches over and flips the power to the speakers, cutting off the rest of the glorious arrest. She leans toward her computer screen, taps a few more keys, and victoriously says, "The recipient of that call is Richard Munford."

Everyone turns to President Alexander to see if he recognizes the name. He nods, providing a brief summary. "Richard Munford, CEO of Munford Aviation and Electronics. Multibillionaire and one of the leading campaign funders for my opponent in the election."

Bebe types again before saying, "It appears he lives on an estate outside of Fredericksburg, but he also has a home in the Keys."

"Shit," Kynan growls. "Where would he have taken her?"

I pinch the bridge of my nose, squeezing my eyes shut in frustration. "Bebe… pull up the houses he owns."

In just mere seconds, she has them up on the screen,

showing us the square footage and geography.

"The Keys' house is in a gated neighborhood. The Virginia estate is isolated on twenty acres and much larger, complete with a few exterior buildings. If I were going to torture someone, I'd put my money there."

I grimace over her casual use of the word *torture*, but she's just speaking plain. We all know what's more than likely happening to Barrett even as we speak.

"Virginia is our play then," I announce.

"We only have one shot at this, Cruce," Kynan points out. "The Keys are closer to where she was kidnapped from."

"I know," I murmur, praying I'm fucking right. But I'm going with a gut instinct I've always trusted. It hasn't let me down yet. "But we need to head to his Virginia estate."

"Let's go then," Kynan says, and we all grab our gear bags from where we'd stowed them around the room. The president has graciously loaned us Marine One, his helicopter, and transport will be quick.

Bebe goes back to her computer. "I'll figure out the best place for you to land nearby, then send the coordinates."

Of course she would. This is what we'd planned once Barrett's kidnapper was identified. She'd direct us to the location, we'd send in a quick reconnaissance, and then we'd storm.

Another hand comes to my shoulder as I make my way to the door. It's Kynan, and he has an expression on his face that is about as far from businesslike as possible. "You okay?" he asks.

"Yeah, shoulder feels fine. No worries."

"Not talking about your shoulder. I'm talking about your state of mind," he replies with a knowing look.

Fuck... he does know how I feel about Barrett.

Before I can respond, he continues. "Remember when I went in and rescued Joslyn?"

I nod, because of course I do. I was there with him. Saw how he wanted to kill the stalker that had taken Joslyn with his bare hands.

"All I'm saying is I've been there," he replies quietly. "I know how fucking scared you are right now, and it's okay. But you have your brothers on your six. We're not going to let you fail. We're going to help you walk Barrett right out of there safe and sound. I promise."

The words are more appreciated than he'll ever know. Because for the first time since Barrett was kidnapped, I feel a glimmer of hope that it will all be okay.

CHAPTER 23

Barrett

I CAN BARELY hear my own screams because my throat is raw and shredded. Still, I'm screaming once again as he presses the cattle prod into my ribs. He never holds it there long—a few seconds at most—but it's enough to send bolts of horrendous pain through me. I can't help but shriek against it. Even when my vocal chords can barely make sound anymore, they still react from the pain.

"Ouch," Paul says with exaggerated empathy. "I know that one really hurt."

I'm panting through the agony, tears streaming down my face. My shoulders are cramping horribly because I'm hanging from the hook and my legs have given way. I've taken several jolts to my thighs. While they ache from the aftereffects, they are rubbery and stopped supporting my weight long ago. Every other spot on my body is throbbing from where he poked me with that damn electric prod.

"Come on, Dr. Alexander," Paul cajoles, putting his

lips near my ear. "Just give it up and all this will stop."

I suck in a few deep breaths, wanting with all my being to just spill my guts. Instead, I say, "Oh, Paul... after all we've been through together, you can call me Barrett."

When he chuckles, I wonder if the fact I've amused him will give me any respite.

It doesn't come from Paul, though, but rather from the door creaking open behind me. I've spun around so many times on this damn hook I've gotten a good 360-degree view of this room. I push to my tiptoes, my feet barking in protest, and I swing myself toward the door.

The old man I'd met upstairs in the study—God, how long ago was that?—stands there with his hands tucked into his pockets. He examines me shrewdly—dispassionately—before turning his gaze to Paul. "Have you made any progress?"

"She's a tough one," Paul says with clear respect in his voice. "But soon... she won't be able to hold out much longer."

"I need faster than 'soon'," the man says as he strides up to us, scanning my body. I'm drenched in sweat and my t-shirt is completely soaked, despite the chill temperatures down here. It's been quite the workout to hold myself up or try to move away from the prod when he strikes out. "I suggest you try an alternative method."

"Understood," Paul says, and a shiver runs up my

spine from the joy in his tone. He's just been given permission to move past this particular form of torture, and I don't want to know what could be worse.

The man nods, turns away, and starts to move to the door.

My mind races, trying to figure out how to buy time. "Wait," I call after him.

He swivels around to stare at me impassively.

"Tell me who you are and why you want my knowledge, and maybe I'll tell you," I say, hoping the promise of information will buy me a conversation, which, in turn, will buy me time.

His ice blue eyes narrow, his lips pressing into a flat line. "You're not in a position to bargain, Dr. Alexander."

"Maybe not," I pant as I start to sag downward, the balls of my feet weakening. "But what do you have to lose? You're going to kill me anyway after all of this, right? Maybe if I knew what you were going to use the knowledge for—if it's for good—I'd give it up a lot faster."

He considers my proposal only briefly before exhaling a small sigh of capitulation. "My name is Richard Munford. My background is in aviation, not energy."

I frown in confusion.

"But I am a passionate and dedicated American. I believe our country will be harmed if President Alexander shares it with others. You asked what my intentions are, and that's my answer. They are pure and simple."

"You're going to destroy it," I say, knowing in my gut that it all boils down to that.

He nods with a grim smile. "I want to know exactly how sound your theory is and the chances of someone else completing it any time soon, which I highly doubt, then yes... I'm going to bury it deep."

"Sharing free energy with the world will bring far more benefits to our country—"

"You may continue," Munford says, but not to me. His eyes are now locked on Paul, effectively cutting my explanation off because he doesn't want to hear it.

"Yes, sir," Paul says, eagerly running the edge of the electric prod along my calf. I jerk in reflex, but he doesn't zap me.

Somehow, I don't think he'll be using it anymore anyway.

Munford moves, but not back to the door. He takes the metal folding chair I'd been in originally, turns it to face me, then lowers himself into it. Casually, he crosses one leg over the other and folds his hands on his lap, watching Paul expectantly with an almost pleasant smile, as if he's getting ready to watch an opera or something.

Sick fuck.

Lips near my ear again, Paul whispers, "Let's have some fun, okay?"

"Fuck off," I growl, earning a zap from the prod to my hip. Another hoarse scream tears free as I jerk away, only to be stopped short the way I'm suspended from the hook.

Rather than cowed, his continual little tortures seem to empower me. I twist my neck to glare over my shoulder. "Keep it coming, asshole. I can take whatever you hand out because you'll get yours one day. Karma is a bitch, and I know she can't wait to take a big fucking bite out of you."

Paul tilts his head back and gives a raucous laugh, once again completely amused by my brass. I'm fairly sure I'm going to die, most likely by being tortured to death. At this point in my life, my greatest regret is I won't get to see it when Karma comes calling on him.

"Last chance," Paul whispers in an almost lover-like tone.

I shudder and try to pull away, but one of his hands comes to my hip to hold me in place. His chin goes to my shoulder—a congenial, friendly type of move—and his tone is conversational. "I know how much pain you can take, Dr. Alexander, and I've been extremely impressed. But I'm curious if you'll perhaps respond better to something different?"

I don't speak because I don't know what he's thinking or has planned. The last thing I want is to spur him into something too quickly.

I study Munford, sitting across from me in his chair with that fucking bland smile as he watches.

Paul's hand moves upward, pulling the edge of my t-shirt along the way. His hand slides over my stomach—fingers spreading to touch as much of my skin as possible. It's an intimate touch—there's no denying that—and my skin crawls as if under attack by a million spiders.

"Maybe," Paul croons softly, turning his head slightly so I can feel his breath on my ear, "I can fuck your secrets out of you."

"No," I whisper in denial. While rape had crossed my mind initially when I'd been kidnapped, I'd later dismissed it when I realized they were working for someone powerful. This was further validated by the fact Paul took immense pleasure in torturing me with pain.

But rape… having a man force himself on me… *into* me… is something I'm not sure I could bear.

Cruce's words seem to ring clear and true within my ears, cutting off Paul and his evil intentions. *You can't give in, Barrett. They will kill you once you give up your knowledge. You hang tough. Stay strong. Believe we will come get you.*

Except I can't.

I saw Cruce get shot, then I never saw him after that. He was stuck in a watery grave, and no one was coming to get me.

Still, I maintain my silence.

"Let's make this a little easier on me," Paul growls. The next thing I know, I'm being lifted with his arm around my belly so he can free my bound wrists from the hook.

"No," I scream. This time, I produce real sound from my shredded vocal chords. Apparently, I still have some fight in me. I start kicking and trying to wrench myself out of his arms, but he easily carries me over to the metal table as if I weighed no more than a feather or was putting up no more effort than a slug.

He slams me down across the top, trapping my arms beneath me. My breath falls short, having been forced from my lungs by the impact of the table, but I still manage to plant my bare feet onto the concrete and push back against him.

Then the cattle prod is slammed down onto the table, inches from my face, and his tone of voice is so cold and filled with evil that I go absolutely still. "I suggest you calm down, Dr. Alexander, or I'm going to fuck you with this instead, and trust me when I say... you won't like it."

Big, salty tears leak out of my eyes as absolute terror and helplessness quell all of my struggling. I suck in a breath and squeeze my eyes shut, telling myself I can bear this torture. That at least if he rapes me with his body rather than the cattle prod, it won't be as painful.

Still humiliating, but it's something I can get through.

In fact, if I just lay there and take it, it will hopefully be over with soon. And it's my struggles that he likes. If I just keep still and quiet, he won't get as much pleasure from it because he likes domination and control. He likes exerting effort to get there, too.

His hands feel cold and slimy as they work at the elastic band of my sweats, his breathing turns heavy as he pushes them down over my hips. Chilly air hits my ass, then the backs of my thighs, and I'm humiliated I'm exposed to not only Paul, but also to Munford as well.

"This might hurt a little," Paul says with what I'd call joyful anticipation, and I hear the zipper on his jeans being lowered.

I swallow hard, grit my teeth, and resolve to survive this.

Except the door to the room flies open with a shrieking groan from the metal hinges. It's done with such force it bangs against the wall. I shift, popping my eyes open, absolutely stunned to see Cruce standing there with a pistol trained right on Paul.

His eyes are hard, unrelenting, and his jaw is locked. For just a brief moment, I figure I must be dreaming.

Or wait... maybe I'm even dead already. Perhaps Paul killed me, and this is some weird type of Heaven that doesn't have bright lights and fluffy white clouds.

However, it does have Cruce so I'm okay with that.

And then Cruce's gaze moves to me for a brief instant—to my exposed body bent over a table—and rage fills his expression.

His eyes snap back toward Paul. Without an ounce of hesitation, he fires his gun once.

Paul doesn't make a sound, but I feel something warm splatter across my backside. By the time I twist the other way to see better, I'm able to catch Paul falling to the ground in my peripheral vision.

I turn back quickly to Cruce, who now has his gun pointed in Munford's direction. He advances on him. I bolt away from the table, jerk my pants up, and pivot to face Cruce so I can watch what he's doing.

"You fucking son of a bitch," Cruce growls as he storms toward Munford, who leans back in his chair and raises both hands in surrender.

I focus on Paul, who is sprawled lifelessly on the floor with open, vacant eyes and a round hole in the middle of his forehead.

Told you Karma was a bitch.

Returning my gaze to Cruce, I see he has reached Munford and now has the gun pressed to his forehead.

"Please, don't," Munford whines, and I can't believe how pathetic and weak he sounds. Just moments ago, he'd been casually watching a woman about to be torture-raped and now he's practically crying like a baby.

"Cruce... don't," someone says from the doorway, and I whirl to see men swarming in. I recognize Saint, but not the others. All wearing black utility pants, black t-shirts, and armed with weapons.

It's my rescue team from Jameson, along with others proclaiming FBI in bright yellow letters on their black jackets.

Saint had called out to Cruce, who is ignoring him. He glares down at Munford. "You don't deserve to live after what you've done. In fact, treason is punishable by death. I'm sure I'd be doing the taxpayers a favor by taking you out, you piece of scum-sucking shit."

"Cruce," Saint says again, softly this time, but it seems to carry more authority. "Can't kill a man in cold blood."

Too bad Saint wasn't in here just a few moments ago. Otherwise, he'd eat those words.

Still, I won't lose a moment's sleep about Paul dying.

I hope Cruce doesn't either.

CHAPTER 24

Cruce

ONE BULLET INTO his brain and Barrett will be avenged. I ended the sick fuck who was getting ready to rape her and probably worse. She looks rough, and there's no telling what he did to her before I got here. Maybe he'd already raped her, and it was done at this sick fuck's behest.

I start to squeeze the trigger and Munford flinches, clamping his eyes shut tightly so as to blot out his executioner's face.

"Cruce… Barrett needs you," Saint's voice manages to penetrate the haze of red fury and vengeance swirling in and around me.

Barrett needs you.

I ease my finger off the trigger to glance over my shoulder. Christ, she looks just fucking awful. Hair sweaty and matted to her head, dried tears on her face, and eyes red with exhaustion and pain. Her wrists are tied in front of her. I didn't miss the hook suspended from the ceiling, nor the cattle prod on the table.

She'd probably been tortured for hours, and I start to put pressure on the trigger again.

"Go to her, brother," Saint urges me. "Take her out of here, and we'll clean up this mess."

I hesitate.

"She needs you," Saint once again says, and those proves to be the words that work. I pull the gun away from Munford, engage the safety, and place it back in my holster.

In three strides, I'm across the room, my hands on Barrett's face so I can try to determine from the depths of her eyes just how bad it was before we rescued her.

"You're alive," she says in awe as her eyes roam over my face. Tears spill from her eyes. "I mean… it's really you. You're alive."

Christ… she'd thought I was dead.

Of course.

Why wouldn't she?

And she'd had that hanging over her heart and her conscience as she took the torture these people bestowed upon her.

"I'm alive," I say, then dip my head to put a grateful kiss on her lips. "We're both alive."

When I pull back, she's freely crying. While I just want to pull her into my embrace and hug all her trauma away, I need those ropes off her more.

"Let me get those off your wrists," I say, letting my

fingers work at the knots while I periodically glance at her face.

Eyes shining and filled with tears—with a mixture of anxiety and relief—yet… she has a dopey smile of wonder as well, and I think it's because I'm very much alive and standing before her. Talk about emotional overload.

As soon as the ropes loosen, I can see her skin has been rubbed raw, bleeding in some areas.

"Where else are you hurt?" I ask, vaguely aware that as I check her out, Saint and crew have pulled Munford out of here while a few FBI agents stand off to the side of the man I'd shot, presumably waiting for the crime scene folks to get here to process stuff.

"I kind of hurt all over," she murmurs, and I snap my gaze to hers.

"Did he… um…"

"Rape me?" she inquires bitterly. When I nod, she shakes her head, and I want to cry in relief. "No… you couldn't have timed your arrival any better."

"What did he do before?" I ask.

Barrett grimaces, her brow furrowing deeply. "Let's just say as an energy scientist, I have a deep aversion to electricity right now, which could be problematic in my career."

God, I want to fucking laugh—bringing humor into such a dark situation—but I can't. Knowing he tortured her with that cattle prod has me wanting to pump a few more bullets into his lifeless body.

"Come on," I say, putting my arm around her shoulder to turn her toward the door. "I need to get you to a hospital—"

"No hospital," she says as she pulls away from me. "I just want to go home."

"Hospital," I reply adamantly. "You need those wounds on your wrists treated, and we need to check out if that prod did any damage. You probably could use some hydration, too."

"No hospital," she replies adamantly. "I've got the betadine, bandages, and Gatorade at home. I just want my own bed, and... I want..."

Her words trail off.

"What do you want?" I ask.

"You," she replies, her eyes locking on mine. "I want you beside me so I can be assured you're real and I'm not hallucinating all of this. And I want a big fat burger and some onion rings. I'll be fine if I can have those things."

I stare a moment before giving a capitulated nod and a short smile. "Okay... I'll take you home."

I lead Barrett up the staircase and out of the basement. Our team had stormed Munford's house not fifteen minutes after we'd arrived, the Marine One helo having landed about a half a mile east. We watched from a copse of trees about fifty yards away, but we really couldn't be sure about anything. We saw two armed men patrolling the grounds, but beyond that, we couldn't tell much else.

With the possibility Barrett was inside and being tortured, we simply couldn't wait. Kynan made a command decision to breach someone's private property without any factual evidence we'd find Barrett there. If he'd been wrong, we'd all face criminal prosecution.

As it stands, we still might. We're a private agency not authorized by law to do what we just did, despite the fact we had FBI backup, but I'll worry about those repercussions later.

Luckily, the two outside guards were easily subdued. There hadn't been anyone in the house when we entered. Bebe had managed to provide the specs on the layout, so when we went in, I chose to go down to the basement, knowing that was the most likely place to find Barrett.

And I walked into a fucking nightmare.

I've never felt such rage before as when I saw Barrett bent over a table, her pants pushed crudely to her knees while a brute of a man unzipped his pants as he stood behind her. The feeling had overwhelmed me for a moment.

And then...

It focused me.

My eyes narrowed, my gun aimed, and there was a tiny imaginary bull's-eye painted on the man's forehead as he had whirled in stunned surprise when I kicked the door open.

I didn't have a moment's hesitation in pulling the trigger, my intention one hundred percent meant to kill.

I'd known it was wrong.

Known I'd saved Barrett from a terrible fate at his hands. Known I could have ordered him to move away from her.

Known that by killing him, I'd become a murderer. Yet, it was the only option I'd had. I'd never be able to live with myself if I let Barrett's pain and torture go unavenged.

On the main floor, we're met by FBI agents and local police as they start to fill the house for processing. No one stops us as I lead her out.

No one looks twice at us.

Until we make it down the front porch steps, my arm still locked tight around Barrett's shoulders, and come face to face with Kynan and Willis Henry, the director of the FBI.

Both wear concerned expressions, which I know has everything to do with the dead body in the basement. That shooting happened less than five minutes ago, but they've already been informed I'd killed a man.

What else did they know about it?

"Mr. Britton," Director Henry says gravely. "We're going to need to talk to you about what happened down there. I'm going to ask you go with two of my agents back to our offices in Washington."

I don't dare look at Kynan, but I can feel the tension rolling off him. "Can this wait?" I ask, nodding to Barrett as I pull her in closer. "She's had a very traumatic experience, and I want to get her home."

"We'd be happy to help arrange transport for Ms. Alexander to either a hospital or to her home—"

"I don't want to go to a hospital," Barrett interrupts, her voice sounding a little shrill. "And I want Cruce to take me home. I'm sure you can appreciate what I've been through, and you can always talk to Cruce tomorrow."

"This is a criminal investigation, Ms. Alexander," the director answers cautiously. "I cannot begin to imagine what you suffered, and we'll obviously need your statement, too. I can have an agent accompany you to save you a trip to our offices."

"I think your 'criminal' investigation needs to be focused on the actual criminals," Barrett snaps hotly. "You know... the man who had me kidnapped and tortured. Richard Munford."

Director Henry's gaze moves from Barrett to me. "Mr. Munford is saying you shot his employee in cold blood. That he was unarmed and helpless."

"He tortured me for hours with an electric cattle prod," Barrett snarls, pulling away from my embrace and getting in Henry's face. "He was getting ready to rape me, and he had just threatened to shove that cattle prod inside me. You should be giving Cruce a medal."

I actually go dizzy upon hearing this.

He had threatened to rape her with that fucking electrified stick?

"That fucker deserved the bullet between his eyes," I growl at the director.

"Jesus Christ," Kynan mutters as he pinches the bridge of his nose.

"I think you need to come with me," Director Henry says with a resigned sigh.

"Wait," Barrett says shrilly, moving to put herself in between me and the director of the FBI. She even holds her arms stretched out as if she could physically keep us apart if either of us didn't want that space. The wounds on her wrists are glaring, and I, in turn, glare at Henry for even attempting this shit while Barrett clearly needs to be taken care. "How can you even do this? What in the hell is wrong with you? Cruce did nothing but protect me and my knowledge. He's an American patriot, and you should be ashamed of yourself."

"Easy there, Barrie," a deep voice says from behind us, and I jolt when I recognize it as the president's. I turn to see him. He's staring at Barrett as if he's on the verge of tears.

Director Henry stands straighter, puffing his chest

out slightly as Barrett pushes past me to move into her uncle's arms. He hugs her tightly, squeezing his eyes shut, and she starts crying again.

His eyes pop open, pinned directly on Willis Henry, and a hard resolve tightens the president's jawline.

He presses a kiss to the top of Barrett's head, then gently pushes her into my arms. I gather her close while the president puts his arm on the director's shoulder and leads him a few feet away.

I can't hear exactly what's being said, so I focus on Kynan. "How fucked am I?"

"I have no clue," he replies with a worried expression. "But that little comment about the man deserving a bullet between his eyes didn't help."

It was the truth, but yeah… should have kept that to myself.

"You going to lecture me on being so irresponsible?" I ask.

"Nope," he says without hesitation.

"Going to fire me?"

Kynan rolls his eyes. "No need. You'll probably be in prison."

Barrett jerks at that, whipping around to Kynan. "No. They can't."

"They can," I murmur, and she pushes out of my embrace with a glare. "You know I didn't have to kill that man, Barrett. But I did, and I'd do it again even knowing the consequences. What he was about to do to you and imagining what he'd already done... I just... I couldn't let that go."

She shakes her head, not wanting to listen.

"You remember what we talked about on the boat that day?" I ask. It takes a moment for realization to set in, but then she gives me a tentative nod.

"We talked about regrets," I remind her, although she's right there with me. I can see it. "And I don't regret this, Barrett. Please know, no matter what happens, killing that man is something I will never regret."

"It's not fair," she cries out, flinging herself into my arms, burying her face in my chest. Pressing my lips to the top of her head, I hold her. Let her cry it out. Trying to shove down the realization I might not ever get to hold her again.

Kynan makes a rough coughing sound, obviously fake. When I raise an eyebrow, his eyes flick over to where the president had just been talking to Directory Henry.

But Henry's gone, and the president watches me hold his niece with a weird expression on his face. A little perplexed, a little affronted, a little resigned, but mixed with a slight tinge of happiness.

He moves toward us, and I give Barrett a tiny squeeze before placing my hands on her shoulders to push her slightly away from me. When she sees her uncle approaching, she immediately starts to implore. "Please, Uncle Jon... can't you do—"

The president holds up his hand in a signal for silence, and Barrett immediately quiets. He looks left and then right, making sure there's no one standing nearby. His Secret Service detail is a good ten yards off, watching us but outside of hearing range.

He steps in closer. In a voice so low I can barely hear him, he says, "I just called in the biggest favor of my career. Cruce... you're free to go. I'd appreciate it if I can leave Barrett in your care while I stay here to monitor things."

Holy shit.

He just pulled me right out of a murder investigation.

Gave me a free pass for killing that man.

Barrett gapes at me in stunned silence a moment before slowly turning to her uncle. His eyes stay locked on me, though, and his voice is rough with emotion. "Cruce... that's twice you've gone above and beyond for me. First, you saved my life, then you saved Barrett's. I can never repay you, but if you think of any way I can—"

"You already did, sir," I say with a nod of my head. He'd just absolved me of murder. "We're absolutely even."

The president reaches out, then touches his fingers to Barrett's cheek. They share an exchanged look of love and gratitude. He then smiles before pivoting on his foot to walk away.

Grinning, Kynan winks before following the president.

Together, Barrett and I watch the bustle of federal and state authorities swarming the estate. I reach down, gently take her hand.

Barrett pins me with a soft, questioning smile.

"Let's go find transport to D.C. so we can get you a burger and some onion rings," I suggest.

Her smile notches up to mega-wattage. "Sounds like the best plan I've ever heard."

CHAPTER 25

Barrett

I COME AWAKE slowly, smiling as I stretch my body. It's been three days since Cruce rescued me. The first thing I do upon conscious awareness of each new day is smile. I'm so grateful I'm alive and in bed next to the man who has quickly become my everything.

Blinking my eyes, I take him in.

He's on his back, hands tucked behind his head as he stares at my ceiling. Of course he's awake, because he always rises before me. Which concerns me, because he's not been sleeping well. Restless, tossing and turning. He'll wake up, lean over me, and watch me in the dark. Sometimes, he touches my face. I don't let him know I'm awake.

I drag my eyes down Cruce's body. His chest is naked, but I know he has on his boxers under the sheet he has pulled up to his waist. There's a bandage over his wound under his left clavicle, a painful reminder of all he went through to save me.

He hasn't tried to make a move on me once, either

too worried about how I'll react or simply because he's not attracted to me anymore. Maybe what we had built during those precious island days wasn't real. Heightened by stress and danger, perhaps we'd bonded over things that weren't grounded in reality, which maybe weren't strong enough to last in normal life.

Reaching a hand out, I move to place it on his chest. For a moment, I'm distracted by the scabbed wounds on my wrist. They feel fine, but they sure are ugly. They're going to leave permanent marks, so I've decided to just accept them as battle scars and leave them as a good reminder of what I can survive.

"Hey," I murmur when he doesn't react to my touch. Just a few days ago, this would have bothered me so much I would have withdrawn. I might not have even had the guts to reach out and touch him, too worried I might be rejected.

But that was the old Barrett who was stuck in a lab working scientific mojo for the greater good. New Barrett had survived kidnapping and torture, and I'm not waiting around to see what life may or may not hand me.

Cruce rolls his head until his eyes lock with mine. His lips curve slightly as he takes me in. "Morning."

I scoot over to him, then put my head on his good shoulder and drape my arm over his stomach. His arm comes around me, holding me close.

Yes, he cares for me. He's never hesitated to show it

in any respect since he walked me out of Munford's house. He's held me close, hugged me, and sweetly kissed me. He's done everything but touch me in the ways I want to be touched.

While in bed with him on Marjorie Island just days ago, I remember wanting to touch him. Dreaming I'd touched him, then making it real.

I shift my arm, sliding my hand over his abdomen and edging it farther south. Cruce tenses and holds his breath while my fingers creep under the sheet.

They move under the elastic band of his boxers, travel through the trimmed, crisp hairs, and right to his cock. Just like I did all those days ago when I'd started all this between us.

Cruce's breath slides out of his mouth in a sigh as I wrap my hand around him. When I tip my head back to look at him, his eyes are closed, bottom teeth dug down into his lip.

I squeeze… stroke.

He groans.

"Feel good?" I ask.

His eyes pop open, travel down to stare for just a moment, then I'm flat on my back and he's on top of me. Mouth on mine, one hand at the nape of my neck and the other at my hip. His erection is pressed solidly between my legs, and I drown in his kiss as I hang onto his shoulders.

Hang on so tight as I feel like I'm on a roller coaster.

Cruce tears his mouth free, eyes fierce. "You okay?"

I frown. "Um... yes. Ready to be better."

"No," he growls with a hard shake of his head. "Are you okay... to do this?"

I blink, confused at first, but then it hits me. He's worried because I was almost raped. Maybe even worried I'm still too fragile from my torture.

Bringing a hand to his face, I rub my thumb through the bristles of his short beard and give him a reassuring smile. "I am more than okay for this. In fact, I really, really need this, Cruce."

Relief fills his eyes, but it's immediately replaced by heat. He touches his lips to mine again, this time so reverently my eyes get a little wet.

I slip my tongue into his mouth and touch it against his, the vibe of the kiss turning a bit dirty. It spurs Cruce on, telling him it's okay to go fast and a little rough if he wants. His hand moves into my panties, fingers gently probing. My hips surge up, legs spread wantonly.

I should be embarrassed about how wet I am when he slips inside me, but I'm not. It's a testament to how much my body belongs to him. That just his kiss does that to me.

Wiggling, I manage to reach down between us... get my hand back around him. He groans into my mouth, and we use our hands on each other until it's unbearable.

Until nothing else will satisfy me except having him inside me.

I release him, pull my mouth away from his, and mutter, "Get your damn underwear off."

My hands are now pushing at the elastic band, and I give a kitteny growl in frustration.

Laughing, Cruce rolls slightly off me. He takes over, pushing his underwear roughly down his legs. I use the moment to take care of my own panties, shucking them down my legs and wriggling out of the stupid, obstructionist things. Then, I whip my t-shirt over my head and toss it to the floor.

I go still as I feel the quiet weight of Cruce's stare.

His eyes roam all over me, my nipples puckering in response to how intense he appears right now.

Like he could devour me.

Cruce seems to bristle with some type of energy as he rolls my way again, settles in between my legs, and puts his hands to the backs of my thighs. I shift, let him spread me wide, and I take him in my grip.

I guide him to me, feel him press and breach me slowly.

A long slide into my body until our pelvises are pressed tightly to one another.

I can't help but groan at the feeling of full completeness. Cruce intently watches where we're joined as his hips pull back, then he slides his long length out almost to the tip before pressing deeply back in.

"Fuck," he grunts, an awed expression washing over his face as he peers down at me. "Feels so fucking good, Barrett."

"So good," I murmur, reaching to palm his face... touch his beard.

One of his hands comes up, takes me by the forearm, and pulls me away so he can examine my scabbed wrists. He dips his head, then places his lips there tenderly before dropping his weight onto me.

Linking our fingers together on both sides, Cruce raises my arms above my head and proceeds to slowly fuck me... torsos pressed together, the only movement his hips as they thrust in and out.

It's slow, luxurious, and consuming.

When his mouth comes back to mine, he fucks me just as sweetly with his tongue.

It goes on and on, and I don't want it to end.

Yet, all good things do, but with Cruce, at least they end with fireworks. We both orgasm hard and slow at the same time. Brutal shudders of ecstasy rip us apart and let us bleed back into each other.

Cruce merely wraps his arms around me, even as we're still shaking, and holds me through it.

♦

"I NEEDED THAT," I murmur, long after we've come

back down to earth. "I needed to know that we're okay."

"Hmmm," he says, sort of an agreeing type of non-statement. I figure the power of speech might still be absent after how hard we both just came.

"I was thinking of going into the office today," I say, and he shifts toward me.

"You sure?" he asks with concern. "I mean… it's only been a few days since—"

"I'm sure," I cut him off. "I sort of need to have some normal me time, too. Sitting around and doing nothing makes me feel a bit weak."

His eyes cloud a little, but he gives a nod to show he understands.

"I'd like someone from Jameson to escort you there and back," he says hesitantly.

"Why?" I ask, shifting so there's some distance between us and I can see him better. "The danger is over, right?"

"Right," he replies, but then he backtracks. "It's just… until the FBI can finish their investigation, we don't know if there are other people out there with the same line of thinking as Munford."

"But I've already given the formula up," I point out. "It's out in the open."

Which is true. I'd turned over all my notes and my laptop to the director of my lab and the scientists representing the United States Department of Energy.

I'd met with them to go over things and explain my theory. I'd been grilled, as I should have been. They'd tested me as best they could, but let's face it… if they'd known all this stuff, they could have figured it out themselves.

"Yes," Cruce counters. "But that's not public knowledge yet."

I sigh in frustration. "How much longer will this have to go on?"

"Until the FBI can finish their investigation," he replies, his tone patient if a bit resigned.

I feel my eyebrows draw inward as something hits me. "Why don't you just escort me?"

Cruce's gaze cuts away from me, but there's a flash of guilt he can't hide. But just as quickly, he gives me his regard again.

The hardening of his jaw is a foreboding tell.

"I need to head back to Pittsburgh," he says. I blink in surprise. It was the last thing I thought I'd hear from him, yet… how could I not consider this?

Cruce doesn't live in D.C. anymore. He has another job in another city. It dawns on me all at once that I've been hiding for the last few days—thinking I was ready to return to normality, while having no clue what that actually meant.

"Oh," I murmur, averting my eyes from Cruce to focus on the bathroom door. Suddenly, I have an overwhelming need to escape this bed.

We'd just re-solidified our intimacy… and for what?

For nothing, I think.

I start to roll away from Cruce, but his arm comes around my waist to stop me. He pulls me back, hand to my chin, and forces me toward him. "I have to get back for a debriefing and to figure out what my next assignment is going to be."

"I understand," I reply woodenly. "And I've got my own stuff to do. All the reactor testing is actually going to be out in California. I'll need to be present for that."

"I know," he replies softly. "It's just a tough time for us right now."

"We'll survive it," I reply brightly.

Cruce studies me with a long hard look deep into my eyes, as if he's trying to fathom what I might mean in those cryptic words. "We'll absolutely survive it. I promise."

A smile plastered to my face, I just stare. I'd survived torture and near rape, so I know I can survive if it doesn't work out between Cruce and me.

Placing my hand on his chest, I lean over and brush my lips lightly against his. When I pull back, I don't bother looking at him. Instead, I roll off the bed with a murmured, "I'm going to take a shower before heading into the lab."

He doesn't reply.

CHAPTER 26

Cruce

I BANG MY fist on the desk, frustrated I can't concentrate on the fucking report I'm supposed to be writing. Kynan's a stickler for paperwork, and I have to recount my entire mission from start to finish in a lengthy document that will get placed in a permanent file.

I suppose that's good news.

I still have a job here at Jameson, which surprises me. Not only had I managed to get our client captured on my watch, but I'd also murdered a man in cold blood because of personal reasons that had nothing to do with safety or self-defense.

That right there was more than enough reason for a justifiable termination if there ever was one, but for some reason... Kynan welcomed me back to headquarters with open arms and a knowing smile.

I know what it means. He'd been in the same exact situation—his woman's tormentor within his grasp and a burning deep in his gut to end his miserable life.

Kynan merely made a different choice than I had,

but it doesn't mean he thinks it was the right choice. I can see within his eyes he has a bit of respect for what I did. Perhaps even a little bit of envy. As it stands, Joslyn's stalker will be in prison for the rest of his life, but that doesn't make Kynan sleep any better at night. He'd prefer the man fade from existence—of that, I have no doubt.

"What did that desk ever do to you?" Saint asks from two desks over. He's been playing a computer game for the last fifteen minutes. Besides that, he's gearing up for a mission he and Kynan have been discussing, yet I have no clue if I'll be called in to help on it or not. It's not been shared with me.

"Nothing," I mutter.

"In a pissy mood because you don't have your girl by your side?" he presses.

I snap my head up with a glare. "Why don't you just play your game and mind your own business? Or better yet, don't you have some new mission to get ready for?"

When Saint grins, I return to my computer screen, trying to orient myself back to the task of completing this summary of events. I'm working on our time together at the island. While I need to report significant things like my daily perimeter checks and equipment monitoring, all I can think about are the precious moments I had with Barrett.

Watching over her while she had her nose pressed

against her laptop screen or in bed with her at night, fighting crazy attraction and lustful dreams. Cooking meals for her and worrying over her.

Taking her out on the boat, watching her fight against relaxation because she just wasn't sure how to do it, but once she got it... she'd been so beautiful and free.

"Seriously... what's going on with you?" Saint says as he sits his ass on the corner on my desk. He's wearing faded jeans and a t-shirt, something that looks completely weird on the guy because if he's not in our working utilityuniform, then he's wearing three-piece suits.

I want to shove him off my desk and tell him to fuck off, but I don't.

I don't because the guy has become a good friend to me over a short period of time. He never hesitated in following me into Munford's house, not knowing if he'd face a hail of bullets or not. He was as committed to saving Barrett as anyone at Jameson.

Sighing, I scrub my hands through my hair and lean back in my chair, which rolls slightly away from the desk. Hands clamped to the armrests, I look up. "I don't know what to do about Barrett."

"What are the choices?" he asks.

"Well, I'm here and she's there," I reply sarcastically. "Not exactly conducive to being together."

"I see your dilemma," he replies, tapping his fingers on my desk. "The heart is a fragile thing. If it's not fed routinely, it forgets how to care. Distance prevents meals, if you know what I mean."

"You're a real romantic," I mutter.

Saint tips his head back, giving a boisterous laugh. When he faces me again, he's still chuckling and shaking his head. "Me? Romantic? The farthest thing from it. I just know facts. Personally, women are devious creatures and aren't to be trusted as far as you can throw them."

Now that has my attention. I blink in surprise. "Are you serious?"

"Dead serious," he says, casually picking at some nonexistent lint on his jeans. He lifts his head up. "But that's just my personal belief. Don't let it influence your path."

"I won't," I murmur, but he does have me intrigued. "So what did she do to you?"

His smile stays in place, but something flashes in his eyes that says I hit the mark. "What makes you think anyone did anything to me?"

"That level of distaste for women either means you've had your heart broken or you had an abusive mother," I point out. Simply psychiatry.

Saint's expression turns hard. "My mother was an angel. The best woman I'll ever know."

I incline my head in acknowledgment, smirking. "Then a woman broke your heart."

"She betrayed me," Saint murmurs, then pushes off

my desk. "Simple as that."

"Barrett's not like that. Not all women are like that."

Shrugging, Saint returns to his desk. He sits in his chair, then spins it slightly toward me. "Probably not. But if you think that way, it makes it easier to stay removed from it. Less dangerous and all."

I lift my chin, understanding what he means. If someone has been burned once, they tend to be shy around the flammable sources. I get it.

My dilemma with Barrett is different, though. I'm not afraid in the slightest that my heart could be at risk with her. In fact, I want it to be so.

But Barrett's life is so radically different from mine. She's a world-famous scientist who will probably end up getting a Nobel prize or some shit for her work. She'll be off traveling the world while I'll still be doing missions for Jameson.

What I do for a living and what she does isn't exactly conducive for a solid relationship.

I study Saint, but his interest is back on his game. He may be jaded and not much help in the romance department, but he did say something that's sticking with me.

Distance can be a killer to a relationship, no matter how hard both parties try. In the two days I've been back in Pittsburgh, Barret and I have kept in close contact. Texts throughout the day and long conversations on the phone that go late into the night. It's reassuring to have that contact.

It's not enough, though.

Not for the long term.

Pushing up from my chair, I make my way through the maze of desks and head to the floating staircase. I take the steps to the gym on the fourth floor two at a time. I'd seen Kynan a little while ago, and he'd said he was on his way there to work out.

Since my return to Jameson two days ago, Kynan has been fairly hands off with me. Basically, he'd reiterated he was glad things had worked out—meaning my absolution of murder charges from as high up as the president—and that Barrett was safe. He'd said he was glad to have me back. That if it hadn't been for my idea to push Scavino into contacting Munford, we most likely would not have found Barrett in time.

It had helped to hear that. Helped to alleviate my guilt over letting her get captured in the first place.

He'd done something that had surprised the shit out of me then.

Clapping a hand on my shoulder, he'd leaned in and said, "Cruce… if you want to stay here at Jameson, you've got to do something for me."

"What's that?" I'd asked.

"You need to admit—and truly mean it—that you know Barrett's kidnapping wasn't your fault."

He'd stunned me so much I'd actually jerked away from him, but he clamped down hard on my shoulder to hold me in place. "Barrett's kidnapping was the kidnapper's fault. In part, Barrett was even at fault. She sent emails out when she'd been specifically told not to. Once they had her location, there was no way you could have withstood that type of strike, even if you'd known it was coming. You did nothing wrong."

I'd just stared.

"Barrett was at fault," Kynan repeated. "And Lord knows… that woman paid tenfold for it. No one deserves what she had done to her, but you don't deserve to have the weight of that on you either. So I'm telling you… if you want to work for me, you better absolve yourself of that shit and do it fast."

Yeah… his words had given me pause. I'm still unsure if I should give them full credence. The depth of my feelings for Barrett won't seem to let me pawn this off on her. I'm the man. I'm the strong one. I should take the blame for her and myself.

Regardless, it's not what I want to talk to Kynan about right now.

In the gym, I find him at the squat rack, loading plates on the barbell. He hears me come in, spares me a glance, and says, "What's up?"

"Got a minute?" I ask as I wind my way through the equipment.

"Sure," he replies. He snags a towel hanging on the rack, then swipes his face with it.

When I reach him, I take a deep breath and let it out. "I hate to do this… but I think I'm going to have to turn in my resignation."

"Jesus fuck, Cruce," Kynan mutters angrily. "I thought I told you to let that shit go. It wasn't your fault, and—"

I shake my head, holding my hand up to silently cut him off. "It's not that. I hear what you're saying about it being on Barrett for sending the email, but that's not why I'm here."

"Then what is it?"

"She's in D.C.," I say. "It's her home, and well… I can't really ask her to come to Pittsburgh. I think her work is far more important than mine, so I'm thinking I want to move to D.C."

Kynan huffs out a breath of dismay. "And what will you do there? If you go back to the Secret Service, you could end up anywhere, although, admittedly… the president would probably give you a plum assignment or something to keep you there."

"I hadn't really thought about it that much," I say truthfully. "Only that while I love this company and the people here, I don't think Barrett can have her career here. So I'm going to have to go there."

Kynan cocks his head thoughtfully, then his eyes

light up. "What if I made your job a little more mobile?"

"What do you mean?" I ask.

"Well, missions are geographical, so whether you two were based here or in D.C., you'd have to travel if you stayed on at Jameson. But otherwise, you could live out of D.C. and travel here as needed. It's not ideal, but fuck, Cruce... I don't want to lose you. You're a fantastic addition to our team."

I hadn't even thought that what he'd just offered could be possible. There's such a unique camaraderie at Jameson, and the bond between the team members can't be discounted. Still, if it lets me keep the best of both worlds—Barrett and a job I really like—then I could make it work.

"I appreciate that," I say, sticking my hand out. He gives it a rough shake before returning to the squat machine.

I pivot, heading for the door.

"Cruce," Kynan calls.

I look over my shoulder.

"If you'd hurry up and finish that fucking report, I'd tell you to hop the next plane out of here to go talk to Barrett about it."

My grin is wide when I nod. "Thanks, boss. Going to do that now."

CHAPTER 27

Barrett

"**I**'M BORED, CAGE." Sighing, I lean my head against the seat and watch the D.C. scenery as he drives me home from work.

"Why's that, doc?" he asks as he casually maneuvers through rush-hour traffic, one hand propped at the top of the steering wheel, his other resting loosely on his thigh.

For the past three days, he's been driving me to and from the lab. During that time, I haven't held back on meaningful conversation with the man. He is, after all, the closest connection I have to Cruce outside our texts and phone calls.

I learned early on Cage doesn't really know Cruce and vice versa. Until recently, Cage has been based out of the Vegas office, while Cruce is new to the organization. I'd point blank asked him that first day how well he knew Cruce, determined to pick his brain hard.

When I realized he wouldn't be much help, I'd still kept talking to him. A loose connection to Cruce was better than none.

I sigh again. "It's just… how do I find work that satisfies me after I've managed to figure out one of the most elusive scientific formulas in humanity's history?"

"Braggart," he replies affectionately, and I shoot him a short smile.

"Seriously," I mutter. "I feel so… useless."

"It's easy." Cage coasts to a stop at a red light, shifting slightly to focus on me. "You find the next elusive formula, then put that gargantuan-sized brain to work on it."

I wrinkle my nose, an automatic reaction to that suggestion.

Cage frowns in response. "Don't you want to do that? Isn't that why you're bored?"

"No." The tone of my voice is slightly whiny. "I want to be bored on a beach or taking a cooking class."

"Yeah," he replies with a shake of his head. His attention returns to the road since the light turns green and traffic starts moving. "That makes no sense whatsoever."

"It's just…" I start off, trying to explain something that doesn't even make sense to me. "It's just that my whole adult life has been devoted to a singular cause. I've spent all my time, exclusive of sleep, working on it. While it fueled and motivated me, and ultimately fulfilled me, I want…"

My words trail off, unable to quite express my angst.

"You want Cruce," Cage fills in the rest.

"No," I say in quick denial. "I mean… yes, of course. But it's more than that."

"You want a life with him," he guesses.

"I want a life," I manage to say. "An all-encompassing one. I want to do the things normal people do. Binge-watch Netflix, take vacations, repaint my cabinets."

"And…" he prompts.

"And I want to be in a relationship," I murmur, shifting closer to him as I give up my deepest desire. "With Cruce. Forever."

Cage's lips curve upward, and he nods at something up ahead. "Now might be your chance to discuss those things."

I jerk my head up to peer out the windshield, my townhome coming into view. Cruce sits on the front steps, and a jolt of exhilaration flows through me. My heart expands and fills with unfettered joy, and yes… I want him forever.

Cage has barely brought the car to a stop at the sidewalk in front of my house before I'm leaping out.

"Later," I call to him, slamming the door before he can reply. I don't even hear him drive off, but I assume he does leave.

Cruce stands from the stoop, then dusts his jeans off. He jogs down the three steps to the sidewalk, barely making it to the bottom before I launch myself at him. He's laughing when my body hits his, and I wrap my legs hard around his waist as I press my face into his neck.

"What are you doing here?" I mumble.

"Came to see a pretty girl to have a serious talk," he replies. Heart starting to hammer, I pull back slightly in question. "Let's sit on the porch, okay?"

I nod, reluctantly letting him lower me until my shoes hit the sidewalk. Cruce takes my hand, leading me up to the landing. We sit down, side by side. He stares down the block in the direction we'd been returning from on our run the morning my first kidnapping attempt happened. It was only a few weeks ago, yet it seems like a lifetime already.

What Cruce and I have been through together makes it feel like I've known this man for an eternity.

I've realized even that's not enough time for me. The only question now is if he feels the same? For all I know, his "serious talk" is to break up with me.

Cruce takes my hand, pulling it over to rest in between his. "It's been a tough few days—being back in Pittsburgh and away from you."

"Same," I admit, reaching over to put my hand on top of our others. I rest my head on his shoulder before saying, "There's been so much craziness. The sudden calm seems like a disconnect. It makes the loneliness worse."

"Have you been lonely?" he asks. "Without me?"

When I nod, he must feel it against his shoulder, because he leans over and presses his lips to the top of my head in a quick kiss. "I've been thinking logistics."

"Of course you have," I reply with a chuckle, lifting my head. "That's your job."

"Logistics about us," he clarifies with a smirk. "This long-distance thing is not going to work for me."

"Me either," I say solemnly. "It's best we break up, right?"

His eyes flare, practically bugging out of his head. "What? No! That's not what I was going to say."

Laughing, I squeeze his hands. "I was joking, and I could tell by the tone of your voice it wasn't what you were going to say. But I am waiting with a little bit of anxiety here... so tell me, what's the big solution for us?"

"I'll move back to D.C.," he says, pulling one of his hands free to bring it to the nape of my neck. He squeezes, then dips his head in closer to me. "I've worked it out with Kynan. I can base myself out of D.C., but I'll have to travel to Pittsburgh some. Of course, I'll have to travel sometimes for other jobs that come my way through Jameson."

I drop my head as I think about his offer. Cruce's fingers come under my chin, forcing my gaze back up. "I thought that would make you happy. You do want to be together, right?"

I nod, smiling through the tears starting to form. "Yes. I want to be together. I love you."

Cruce goes unnaturally still, and I wonder if this was the wrong time to break that news to him. We've known each other just shy of a month, but what we've been through has bonded us closer than most. I've spent more time with Cruce over these last few weeks than I have with most of my friends combined over my lifetime. We've meshed hard and fast and I trust my heart, despite how little practice it has had with this tender feeling.

"Too soon?" I guess with a sheepish expression.

"No," he murmurs, eyes still wide with awe. "Perfect timing, actually. I just… I wasn't sure you felt that way. I know I do. Love you, that is."

"Do you really?" I ask, not because I'm having a tough time believing it, even though this is new and all.

But mainly because it sounded extremely nice, and I want to hear it again.

"I love you," he says candidly, staring deep into my eyes. "I want to be with you forever, whatever that means. I don't want to be in a life without you by my side."

My gaze moves outward across the street, watching the bustle of rush-hour traffic and the pedestrians coming off the Metro a few blocks down.

When I look back at him, I admit, "I've always been so closed off from life and people. I've never been a romantic or dreamy type of woman. Science was my life and my love for so long, but all it took was a few moments with you to realize my life was fundamentally lacking in something important. When I saw you get shot and sink into the water, I'd never known pain like that. My heart was so broken, and I instinctually knew I was suffering the pain of lost love. It's how I figured out I loved you. It's how I realized I was a changed person. Cruce... I don't even know if I could go back to the same life I was leading."

"What are you saying?" he asks tentatively.

I feel like I'm on the brink of metamorphosis. I'm making a gut decision based on feelings churning deep, but I think it's the right thing. "I'm saying I think I want to back away from my work for a bit. I mean... I don't even have any current work to do, but I've already got offers pouring in from all kinds of private corporations and even some governments who want to hire me. But... I don't think I want that."

"What do you want?"

"The dream," I murmur, and my heart skips a beat over the way his expression warms with happiness. "I want you. A family—in our own time, of course. I want to learn how to cook and plant flowers in a backyard. Want to go to sleep with you every night, or as many as possible given your work. I think... I want to move to Pittsburgh with you."

Cruce shifts to angle toward me, his hands coming to my shoulders. He looks hopeful and wary all at the same time. "Are you sure? You're big stuff right now, Barrett. You could go anywhere in this world... command any salary you wanted. Your future is bright and set."

"Not without you, it isn't," I say honestly. "And frankly... right now, I don't want anything but you. I'd like to take a break to just enjoy my life for a bit."

Cruce chuckles. "I bet getting kidnapped and tortured put things into perspective."

I shake my head. "Nothing to do with that. *You* put things into perspective for me."

"I did?" Cruce looks very triumphant right now, his chest puffed out a bit.

"You told me back on the island that when I got involved in my work, you believed the world could burn down around me and I wouldn't even notice. And yes, that was probably true. But who I am now only wants the world to burn down around me with you by my side, because it wouldn't matter as long as we are together."

"I love you," he replies simply, bending his head to get in closer. "Love you more than anything in this world, Barrett. I'll give you whatever you want, but if it's Pittsburgh, then I say let's do it."

"And the dream?"

"I'll give you that, too," he murmurs before moving in to brush a sweet kiss on my mouth. He pulls away, locking his determined eyes on mine. "Promise."

EPILOGUE

Cruce

I POINT THE remote control at the TV, flipping through the channels, but I don't see anything that interests me. As far as comfort goes, this hotel bed has it going on. If I'm not careful, I might doze off, which would ruin the entire evening. I sit up a little straighter, pushing against the pillows I'd stacked against the headboard, and choose a news station that's heavy on opinion and light on fact, knowing it will irritate me enough to at least keep me awake.

Barrett finally exits the bathroom, a waft of steam following. Her wet hair is wrapped in a towel, and she's wearing one of my t-shirts. From personal experience, having lived with her for the last several weeks, I know she won't have any panties on under it.

I glance at the clock, noting I still have a few minutes, then watch as she trudges my way. She makes it to her side of the bed and falls face-first onto the mattress, groaning with extreme exaggeration. "I don't know if I've ever been this tired in my life."

"Preach it, sister," I reply, because I'm feeling the same level of exhausted.

We've just completed the last day of a four-day trip to Orlando, where we've taken in the Magic Kingdom, Epcot, Hollywood Studios, and Universal Studios while under the hot Florida sun. So fucking stupid to come here in the summertime, but I just couldn't let go of the fact Barrett had never been before.

Never been on a frivolously fun vacation ever.

We fly home to Pittsburgh tomorrow. I'm thoroughly whipped, but there is one more thing that must be done.

She twists slightly. "If you want to do sex stuff to me, you better make it fast," she mutters.

I snort because as tired as I am, I'm never too tired to do sex stuff with her. But right now, I have other stuff on my mind.

I roll off my side of the bed, then head toward the mini-fridge I had secretly stocked while we were at Universal today. After I open the door, I pull out a bottle of chilled champagne and two glass flutes.

Barrett lifts her head from the bed with interest. "You know one glass of that will put me out. No sex stuff tonight."

"I'm sure I won't die if we don't fuck on at least one night a week," I reply dryly as I proceed to uncork the bottle.

Giggling, Barrett climbs out of the bed. Truth is that we don't have sex every night, but we damn sure come close to it. We can't get enough of each other, and I'm all right by that.

Pulling the towel off her head, she tosses it on the end of the bed, sauntering toward me as I pour two glasses of champagne at the TV stand. She grabs her glass and holds it up, waiting for me to tap mine against it, but I shake my head and take her free hand.

"Let's go out on the balcony," I say.

Grumbling, she follows me out into the muggy Florida night. "It's so humid… I'm going to need another shower when we go in."

"Damn right you are," I say. "I've got my second wind. Later, I'm going to do sex stuff with you, so you'll definitely need another shower."

Barrett snickers, leaning forward to press her stomach against the railing. We stayed at the Grand Floridian in a room that faces the Magic Kingdom across the water. It's the first evening we even stepped out onto the balcony.

I glance at my watch, then at Barrett. "Have a good time this week?"

She looks away from the Magic Kingdom, swiveling slightly toward me while still holding her glass of champagne. "I've had the absolute best time in my life, and it's all because of you."

"I'm glad," I say, then finally hold my glass of champagne up to her. She clinks hers against mine. When she moves it to her lips to take a sip, I say, "I'd give you anything in the world."

Her glass halts millimeters from her lips, and she smiles. "I'd do the same for you."

"Promise?"

She nods and lowers her glass, head tilted in curiosity.

"Would you marry me?" I ask as I reach into the front pocket of my cargo shorts, then pull out the black box I'd stuffed in there when she went into the bathroom earlier. I'd known I was going to propose to her this week, but I wanted it to be the perfect time. We've been on the run so much since getting here, there hasn't been a great time, but there is now.

Like right now.

The first boom of fireworks cracks the night sky as the sound reaches us before the lights. In the next second, an explosion of fiery speckles fills the area over the castle.

Barrett jumps slightly, whirls to see the array of fireworks filling the air, then gasps. "Oh, wow."

I don't look at them, though.

I only watch her as she takes in the fireworks, still holding her glass of champagne that hasn't been touched, as I wait patiently for her answer.

Luckily, she doesn't make me suffer for long.

Turning back to me, she looks at the box. "Going to open that up?"

"Nope," I say with a grin. "Not until I know what your answer is going to be."

"I don't get to base my answer on the size of the diamond, huh?" she quips with a saucy grin.

Laughing, I shake my head.

"In that case," she drawls, pausing to finally takes a delicate sip of her champagne to drag the moment out. "I think my answer will be 'yes'."

My hands are occupied with a ring and a champagne flute, which is not convenient at all. I hurry to set them both on the small patio table flanked by two chairs, then pull Barrett into my arms. She tips her head back, already anticipating my kiss, and I can see her smiling as I bring my mouth to hers.

It's fucking perfect.

This night is perfect.

She's perfect.

She said yes, and my life is perfect.

When I pull back, I ask, "Want to see the ring?"

Barrett shrugs. "I guess."

I kiss her again, until she finally starts making a grab for the box, then I open it with a flourish.

The diamond inside is massive, and I'd expected the gasp that comes out of her mouth. It's so big, in fact, I can see the reflection of the fireworks in its surface.

"Oh, Cruce," she murmurs, her voice shaking. "That's way too much."

"Nothing is too much for you," I assure her as I pluck it from its resting spot and take her left hand in mine. When I slide the ring onto her finger, my first indication she's crying is a tear splashing on the back of my hand as she bends to marvel over it.

"Hey, no tears," I admonish gently. Inside, though, I'm secretly warmed to my fucking toes that she's crying with joy over this moment.

I want to give her the dream we've talked about. I want to give her everything because she's already given it to me. And by everything, I mean her heart.

Barrett looks up, dashing the tears away with the back of her hand. "I love you, Cruce. You've made me so happy."

"I love you, too," I say before I kiss her yet again.

The fireworks boom and shake the ground, the lights sparkle, and the world seems to burn around us.

But neither one of us notices.

The suspense continues at Jameson Force Security! GO HERE to preorder Code Name: Heist (Jameson Force Security, Book #3), coming January 7, 2020!

sawyerbennett.com/bookstore/code-name-heist

Go here to see other works by Sawyer Bennett:

https://sawyerbennett.com/bookshop

Don't miss another new release by Sawyer Bennett!!! Sign up for her newsletter and keep up to date on new releases, giveaways, book reviews and so much more.

https://sawyerbennett.com/signup

Connect with Sawyer online:

Website: sawyerbennett.com

Twitter: twitter.com/bennettbooks

Facebook: facebook.com/bennettbooks

Instagram: instagram.com/sawyerbennett123

Book+Main Bites:

bookandmainbites.com/sawyerbennett

Goodreads: goodreads.com/Sawyer_Bennett

Amazon: amazon.com/author/sawyerbennett

BookBub: bookbub.com/authors/sawyer-bennett

About the Author

Since the release of her debut contemporary romance novel, Off Sides, in January 2013, Sawyer Bennett has released multiple books, many of which have appeared on the New York Times, USA Today and Wall Street Journal bestseller lists.

A reformed trial lawyer from North Carolina, Sawyer uses real life experience to create relatable, sexy stories that appeal to a wide array of readers. From new adult to erotic contemporary romance, Sawyer writes something for just about everyone.

Sawyer likes her Bloody Marys strong, her martinis dirty, and her heroes a combination of the two. When not bringing fictional romance to life, Sawyer is a chauffeur, stylist, chef, maid, and personal assistant to a very active daughter, as well as full-time servant to her adorably naughty dogs. She believes in the good of others, and that a bad day can be cured with a great work-out, cake, or even better, both.

Sawyer also writes general and women's fiction under the pen name S. Bennett and sweet romance under the name Juliette Poe.

2/28/20

CPSIA information can be obtained
at www.ICGtesting.com
Printed in the USA
LVHW082205240120
644730LV00016B/379

9 781947 212541